Usborne

100 yummy things to cook & eat

Contents

To: Maidenhead Library
SELMS: Windsor and Maidenhead
Intransit Item

Branch: Boyn Grove Library
Date: 3/12/2022   Time: 3:08 PM

Item: 100 yummy things to eat
        38060000000788

From: Boyn Grove Library

Fairy cakes

Makes 12 cakes

For the cakes:
90g (3½oz) self-raising flour
90g (3½oz) soft margarine
90g (3½oz) caster sugar
2 medium eggs
½ teaspoon vanilla essence

For the icing:
175g (6oz) icing sugar
1½ tablespoons warm water
yellow food dye
small sugar flowers

a 12-hole shallow bun tray
paper cake cases

🌸 Store in a single layer in an airtight
container for up to 3 days.

The mixture should reach a little higher than half way up in each case.

1. Heat the oven to 190°C, 375°F, gas mark 5. Put a paper case into each hole in the tray. Sift the flour into a bowl.

2. Add the margarine, sugar and vanilla. Break the eggs into a cup, then add them to the bowl. Stir until the mixture is creamy.

3. Use a teaspoon to divide the mixture between the paper cake cases. Bake the cakes for 15 minutes, until they are firm and golden.

4. Wear oven gloves to take the cakes out of the oven. Leave them in the tray for a few minutes. Lift them onto a wire rack.

5. Sift the icing sugar into a bowl. Stir in the warm water to make a smooth white paste. Use a teaspoon to ice four of the cakes.

6. Add two drops of yellow food dye to the icing and stir it in well. Use a teaspoon to ice four more cakes.

7. Add two more drops of yellow dye and stir it in well. Spread it onto the last four cakes. Use sugar flowers to decorate the cakes.

Oranges and lemons

To make about 24 oranges and lemons,
you will need:

350g (12oz) icing sugar
1 small orange
3 teaspoons of egg white,
   mixed from dried egg white
   (mix as directed on the packet)
red and yellow food dye
1 lemon
a baking sheet lined with
   greaseproof paper

♣ These sweets need to
be eaten within 10 days.

Use the small holes on a grater.

Use a lemon squeezer.

1. Sift half the icing sugar through a sieve into one bowl, and half into another. Grate the skin from half of the orange.

2. Cut the orange in half and squeeze it. Put five teaspoons of the juice into a bowl. Add 1½ teaspoons of egg white.

3. Add the grated orange, two drops of yellow food dye and one drop of red food dye to the bowl. Mix everything well.

Squeeze the mixture until it is smooth.

The marks make the outsides look like orange skin.

4. Add the mixture to one of the bowls of icing sugar. Stir it with a blunt knife, then squeeze it with your fingers.

5. Make about 12 orange balls on a clean work surface dusted with icing sugar. Roll the balls over the small holes on a grater.

6. Grate about half of the lemon's skin. Cut the lemon in half. Squeeze it and put five teaspoons of the juice into a bowl.

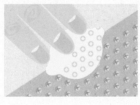

7. Add 1½ teaspoons of egg white, a few drops of yellow food dye and the grated lemon to the bowl. Mix everything together.

8. Stir the juice mixture into the other bowl of icing sugar. Make lemon shapes and roll them over the small holes on a grater.

9. Put the sweets onto the baking sheet. Leave them for a few hours to become firm. Keep them in an airtight container.

Little pastries

To make 24 little pastries, you will need:
375g (13oz) package ready-rolled puff pastry, taken out
  of the refrigerator 15-20 minutes before you start.
1 medium red onion
1 tablespoon olive oil
a pinch of salt and of ground black pepper
½ teaspoon Italian seasoning
150g (5oz) mozzarella cheese
12 cherry tomatoes, washed
1 tablespoon milk
2 greased baking trays

Heat your oven to 220°C, 425°F,
gas mark 7, before you start.

✿ Cool for 5 minutes before eating.

Stir the onion as it cooks.

1. Using a sharp knife, cut the ends off the onion. Peel it, then cut it in into quarters. Slice each quarter finely.

2. Put the sliced onion into a frying pan with the olive oil. Gently cook the onion on low heat for about 5 minutes.

3. Take the pan off the heat. Stir in the salt and pepper and the seasoning. Then, unroll the pastry and cut it into 24 squares.

4. Put the squares onto the baking trays, leaving spaces between them. Prick the middle of each square twice with a fork.

5. Put the mozzarella onto a cutting board. Cut the mozzarella into tiny cubes, then cut the cherry tomatoes in half.

6. Pour the milk into a mug. Then, brush milk around the edge of each square, making a border about 1cm (½in) wide.

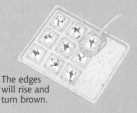

The edges will rise and turn brown.

7. Spoon some of the onion mixture onto each pastry square. Make sure that you don't cover the milk border.

8. Put half of a tomato onto each square, then scatter a few cubes of mozzarella on top of each one.

9. Cook the pastries for 12-15 minutes. Lift them off the baking trays with a spatula and leave them to cool for 5 minutes.

Lace biscuits

Makes 16 biscuits

For the biscuits:
75g (3oz) butter
75g (3oz) porridge oats
100g (4oz) caster sugar
1 medium egg
2 teaspoons plain flour
1 teaspoon baking powder

For the lime cream filling:
1 lime
250g (9oz) mascarpone
cream
25g (1oz) icing sugar

✿ Serve as soon as possible,
or within two hours.

Draw around the baking trays and cut out the shapes.

1. Heat the oven to 170°C, 325°F, gas mark 3. Cut out two rectangles of baking parchment and line two baking trays.

2. Put the butter into a pan over a low heat until the butter has melted. Take it off the heat. Stir in the oats with a wooden spoon.

3. Stir the sugar into the mixture. Then leave it to stand for two or three minutes to let the butter soak into the oats.

4. Break the egg into a bowl and beat it with a fork. Stir it into the mixture. Sift in the flour and baking powder.

5. Put four heaped teaspoons of mixture onto each tray. Make sure they are well spaced out. Bake them for 9-10 minutes.

6. Leave the biscuits to cool for five minutes. Carefully lift them off the paper with a blunt knife and onto a wire rack.

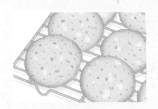

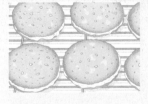

7. Leave the parchment on the trays. Follow steps 5 and 6 to bake more biscuits. Leave all the biscuits on the rack to cool.

8. For the filling, grate the rind of the lime and mix it with the mascarpone. Sift over the icing sugar. Mix all the ingredients.

9. Spread some lime cream onto one biscuit. Put another biscuit on top. Then, sandwich together all the biscuits.

Chocolate-dipped fruit

You will need:
450g (1lb) small strawberries,
  with their stalks left on
75g (3oz) milk chocolate drops
75g (3oz) white chocolate drops
a piece of baking parchment,
  on a large plate

✿ Eat the chocolate-dipped
fruit on the day you make it.

You could dip
segments from
a satsuma in
chocolate, too.

1. Put the strawberries into a sieve. Then, rinse them under cold running water for a little while, to remove any dirt.

2. Dab the strawberries with a paper towel, to remove most of the water. Then, spread them out on a plate to dry.

3. Fill a large saucepan a quarter full of water. Heat it until the water bubbles, then remove the pan from the heat.

4. Put the milk chocolate drops into a heatproof bowl. Wearing oven gloves, carefully put the bowl into the pan.

5. Stir the chocolate with a wooden spoon, until it has melted. Using oven gloves, carefully lift the bowl out of the water.

6. Melt the white chocolate drops in the same way. Leave both bowls of chocolate to cool for 2 minutes.

7. Dip a strawberry halfway into the melted chocolate. Then, lift it out again and let it drip over the bowl.

8. Lay the strawberry on the baking parchment on the plate. Dip the other strawberries, then put them into a fridge to set.

9. After about 20-30 minutes, carefully peel the strawberries off the paper. Then, put them back onto the plate.

Shortbread

To make 8 wedges of shortbread, you will need:
150g (5oz) plain flour
25g (1oz) ground rice or rice flour
100g (4oz) butter, refrigerated
50g (2oz) caster sugar
a 20cm (8in) shallow round tin

Heat your oven to 170°C, 325°F,
gas mark 3, before you start.

❋ Keep in an airtight container
and eat within 5 days.

1. To grease the tin, dip a paper towel into some butter. Rub the paper towel all over the inside of the tin.

2. Pour the flour and ground rice or rice flour into a sieve over a large bowl. Shake the sieve to sift them into the bowl.

3. Cut the butter into small pieces. Add them to the bowl, then mix them in with a blunt knife, to coat them with flour.

4. Using your fingertips, rub in the pieces of butter. Lift the mixture and let it fall back into the bowl as you rub.

5. Keep rubbing in the butter until the mixture looks like breadcrumbs. Then, stir in the sugar with a wooden spoon.

6. Holding the bowl in one hand, squeeze the mixture into a ball. The heat from your hand will make it stick together.

Cut along the lines again, then lift out the shortbread.

7. Press the mixture into the tin with your fingers. Then, use the back of a spoon to press down the top and make it level.

8. Press a pattern around the edge with the prongs of a fork. Then, use a blunt knife to cut the mixture into eight wedges.

9. Bake the shortbread for 30 minutes, until it is golden. Leave it for 5 minutes, then lift it onto a wire rack to cool.

Vegetable stir-fry

To make a stir-fry for 4 people,
you will need:
2 courgettes
1 red or yellow pepper
1 carrot
100g (4oz) baby sweetcorn
100g (4oz) mangetout
4 spring onions
2-3 tablespoons of vegetable oil
1 clove of garlic, crushed
100g (4oz) fresh beanshoots

For the sauce:
1 teaspoon of cornflour
1 tablespoon of light soy sauce
2 tablespoons of water
2 tablespoons of cooking oil
a pinch of sugar

✿ Eat straight away, on its own
or with boiled rice or noodles.

1. Cut the ends off the courgettes. Cut them in half, then into strips. Cut the strips into pieces about 5cm (2in) long.

2. Cut the ends off the pepper and cut it in half. Scrape out the seeds and white bits inside, then cut it into thin slices.

3. Peel the carrot, then cut off the ends. Slice it finely. Then, cut the ends off the sweetcorn and cut them in half lengthways.

4. Using clean kitchen scissors, snip the ends off the mangetout. Then, cut each mangetout into several smaller pieces.

5. Cut the ends off the spring onions. Remove the outer layer, then cut the onions diagonally into 5cm (2in) slices.

6. Put the cornflour into a cup. Mix it with a few drops of water, to make a paste. Stir in the rest of the sauce ingredients.

Stir the vegetables quickly with a wooden spoon.

Keep stirring the vegetables as they cook.

7. Heat the oil in a frying pan or wok on a medium heat. Add the courgettes, pepper and carrot, then cook them for 3 minutes.

8. Add the sweetcorn, garlic and spring onions. Cook them for a minute, then add the mangetout and beanshoots.

9. Cook everything for 3 minutes. Then, stir the sauce and pour it into the pan. Stir it in well, to coat all the vegetables.

Marshmallow fudge

To make about 36 pieces of fudge,
you will need:
450g (1lb) icing sugar
100g (4oz) white marshmallows
100g (4oz) unsalted butter
2 tablespoons of milk
half a teaspoon of vanilla essence
an 18cm (7in) shallow square cake tin

❀ Store in an airtight container in a
fridge and eat within a week.

1. Lay the tin on a piece of greaseproof paper. Draw around it, then cut out the square, just inside the line.

2. Using a paper towel, wipe cooking oil all over the inside of the tin. Press in the paper square and wipe oil over it, too.

3. Sift the icing sugar through a sieve into a large bowl. Make a hollow in the middle of the sugar with a spoon.

Use a wooden spoon.

4. Using clean scissors, cut the marshmallows in half. Put them into a small saucepan with the butter, milk and vanilla.

5. Gently heat the pan on a low heat, until everything has melted. Stir the mixture every now and then.

6. Pour the mixture into the hollow in the icing sugar. Stir everything together really well, until the fudge is smooth.

Use a spoon to flatten the top of the fudge.

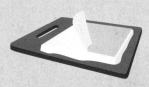

7. Put the fudge into the tin and push it into the corners. Leave it in the tin to cool, then chill it in a fridge for 3 hours.

8. Loosen the edges of the fudge with a blunt knife. Then, turn it out onto a chopping board and peel off the paper.

9. Carefully cut the fudge into 36 pieces, using a sharp knife. Then, put it back into the fridge for an hour to harden.

Tiny pink cookies

To make about 65 tiny cookies, you will need:
50g (2oz) butter, softened
25g (1oz) icing sugar
quarter of a teaspoon of red food colouring
1 teaspoon of milk
quarter of a teaspoon of vanilla essence
75g (3oz) plain flour
little star and heart cutters
2 baking trays, wiped with cooking oil
a cocktail stick

Heat your oven to 180°C, 350°F,
gas mark 4, before you start.

❀ Store the cookies in an
airtight container and eat
them within a week.

You could decorate
the cookies by dusting
them with icing sugar
when they are cool.

1. Put the butter into a bowl and stir it until it is creamy. Sift in the icing sugar, then stir the mixture until it is smooth.

2. Add the red food colouring and stir it in. When the mixture is pink, add the milk and the vanilla essence.

3. Sift the flour into the bowl and mix everything well. Then, squeeze the mixture in your hands, to make a ball of dough.

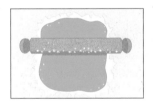 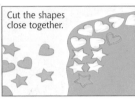 

Cut the shapes close together.

4. Dust a rolling pin and a clean work surface with a little flour. Then, roll out the dough, until it is about 5mm (¼in) thick.

5. Use the cutters to cut out lots of shapes from the dough. Then, lift the shapes onto the baking trays with a spatula.

6. Squeeze the scraps to make a ball, then roll it out again. Cut out more shapes, then put them onto the baking trays.

Wear oven gloves.

7. Push the end of a cocktail stick into some of the cookies, to make patterns. Don't worry if it goes all the way through.

8. Bake the cookies for 6-8 minutes. Carefully lift them out of the oven, then leave them on the baking trays to cool.

Chocolate crunchies

To make about 25 chocolate crunchies, you will need:
75g (3oz) rich tea biscuits
50g (2oz) dried apricots
225g (8oz) white, milk or plain chocolate drops
4 tablespoons of golden syrup
1 teaspoon of drinking chocolate or icing sugar
small paper cases

❋ Store in an airtight container in a fridge
and eat within 3 days.

1. Break the biscuits into tiny pieces and put them into a bowl. Then, cut the apricots into tiny pieces. Add them to the biscuits.

2. Fill a saucepan a quarter full of water and heat it until the water bubbles. Then, remove the pan from the heat.

3. Put the chocolate drops into a heatproof bowl. Then, wearing oven gloves, carefully put the bowl into the pan.

Wear oven gloves.

4. Stir the chocolate until it has melted. Carefully lift the bowl out of the water. Let the chocolate cool for a minute.

5. Quickly stir in the golden syrup, then add the biscuits and apricots. Mix everything well with a wooden spoon.

6. Scoop up some of the mixture with a teaspoon. Using your hands, roll it into a ball. Then, put the ball into a paper case.

7. Make more balls from the mixture. Put them onto a plate, then chill them in a fridge for an hour, to go firm.

8. Sift drinking chocolate over white chocolate crunchies, or icing sugar over milk or plain chocolate crunchies.

Lamb kebabs

To make kebabs for
4 people, you will need:

For the marinade:
1 tablespoon of fresh lemon juice
a large pinch of dried oregano
4 tablespoons of olive oil
1 clove of garlic, crushed
a pinch of salt and of ground black pepper

For the kebabs:
2 large boneless lamb steaks, each
  weighing about 175g (6oz)
1 red onion
1 red pepper
2 courgettes
8 kebab or satay sticks (if you're using
  wooden sticks, soak them in a dish of
  water to stop them burning under the grill)

Take the pieces of lamb
and vegetables off the
sticks, then serve with
pitta bread and lettuce.

❀ Eat the kebabs straight away.

24

Use a sharp knife.

The marinade will make the lamb tender and tasty.

1. For the marinade, put the lemon juice, oregano, olive oil, garlic, salt and pepper into a large bowl. Stir everything well.

2. Carefully trim the fat off the lamb. Then, cut the lamb into 2cm (¾in) cubes. Mix the cubes into the marinade.

3. Cover the bowl with plastic foodwrap and put it into a fridge for at least an hour. Meanwhile, prepare the vegetables.

Throw away the ends of the courgettes.

4. Peel the onion and cut it into quarters. Then, cut across each quarter. Separate each chunk into double slices, like this.

5. Cut the ends off the pepper. Remove the seeds and cut it into 2cm (¾in) squares. Then, cut the courgettes into thick slices.

6. Carefully push one cube of lamb onto each kebab or satay stick. Be careful of the sharp end of the sticks.

You will need the leftover marinade in step 8.

The kebabs should be about 8cm (3in) below the grill.

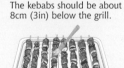

Be careful – the grill pan will be very hot.

7. Push all the vegetables and pieces of lamb onto the sticks. Then, heat the grill to a medium heat, for 5 minutes.

8. Put the kebabs onto the rack in a grill pan. Brush them with some marinade, then grill them for 10 minutes.

9. Turn the kebabs over. Spoon the rest of the marinade over them. Grill them for 5-10 minutes, or until they are browned.

Marzipan toadstools

To make 8 marzipan toadstools,
you will need:
250g (9oz) 'white' marzipan*
3 drops of red food colouring

❀ Store the toadstools in an airtight container
and eat them within 2 weeks.

You could make a
mixture of big and
small toadstools.

*Marzipan contains ground
nuts, so don't give these to
anyone who is allergic to nuts.

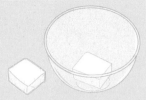

1. Cut the block of marzipan in half with a sharp knife. Then, wrap one half in plastic foodwrap and put the other half into a small bowl.

2. Add the food colouring to the bowl. Mix it into the marzipan with your fingers. Then, break the red marzipan into eight pieces.

Wash your hands before you handle the 'white' marzipan.

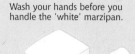

3. Roll each piece into a ball, then squash the balls to make toadstool tops. Use your thumb to make a hollow in the bottom of each one.

4. Unwrap the other half of the marzipan. To make spots, break off a third of the marzipan and roll it into lots of little balls.

5. Press several little balls onto each toadstool top. Then, break the remaining piece of marzipan into eight pieces, for the stalks.

6. To make the stalks, roll each piece of marzipan between your fingers. Gently press a spotty toadstool top onto the top of each stalk.

Chocolate nests

To make 10 chocolate nests, you will need:
225g (8oz) plain chocolate
50g (2oz) butter
2 tablespoons of golden syrup
100g (4oz) corn flakes
30 chocolate mini eggs
paper cake cases
a baking tray with 12 shallow holes

❋ Store in an airtight container in a fridge
and eat within 3 days.

The syrup will slide off the hot spoon.

1. Put 10 paper cases into the holes in the baking tray. Then, break up the chocolate and put it into a large saucepan.

2. Cut up the butter and add it to the pan. Then, dip a tablespoon into hot water and use it to add the golden syrup.

3. Gently heat the pan on a low heat, until the butter and chocolate have melted. Stir the mixture all the time.

Try not to crush the corn flakes.

Push the flakes up the sides of the paper cases.

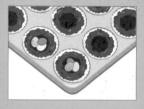

4. Turn off the heat, then add the corn flakes to the pan. Gently stir them into the chocolate, until they are coated all over.

5. Using a teaspoon, fill the paper cases with the chocolate mixture. Make a hollow in the middle of each nest with the spoon.

6. Put three mini eggs into each nest. Then, put the nests into a fridge and leave them for about an hour to harden.

Pancakes

To make about 12 pancakes, you will need:
100g (4oz) plain flour
a pinch of salt
1 egg
1 tablespoon of sunflower oil
300ml (½ pint) milk
sunflower oil, for wiping

✿ Eat the pancakes straight away, while they
are hot. Eat them with golden or maple syrup,
or lemon juice and caster sugar.

1. Put the flour and salt into a sieve, over a large bowl. Shake the sieve until all the flour has fallen through.

2. Press a spoon into the middle of the flour, to make a hollow. Break an egg into a cup, then pour it into the hollow.

3. Add the tablespoon of oil and 2 tablespoons of milk. Use a whisk to start mixing the egg, oil and milk with the flour.

4. Add some more milk and mix it with more of the flour. Repeat this until all the milk is mixed in and the batter is smooth.

5. Put 2 tablespoons of oil into a cup, for wiping. Then, heat a small frying pan on a medium heat for about a minute.

6. Dip a paper towel into the oil and quickly wipe it over the bottom of the pan. Don't touch the hot pan with your fingers.

Use a spatula to loosen and flip the pancake.

7. Add 3 tablespoons of batter, then take the pan off the heat. Then, carefully swirl the batter around to make a circle.

8. Put the pan on the heat. Cook the batter for about a minute, until it is pale and lightly cooked, with little holes on top.

9. Loosen the edge of the pancake, then flip it over. Cook it for 30 seconds, then slide it onto a plate. Make more pancakes.

Mixed salad

To make a salad for 4 people, you will need:

For the salad:
2 little gem lettuces or a cos lettuce
half a cucumber
225g (8oz) baby plum or cherry tomatoes
2 medium carrots

For the lemon and honey dressing:
5 tablespoons of sunflower oil
1½ tablespoons of lemon juice
1 teaspoon of clear honey
a pinch of salt and of ground black pepper

✿ Eat straight away, or
serve it as part of a meal.

Use a serrated knife.

1. Pull the leaves off the lettuces. Rinse them well in cold water, shake them dry, then tear them into pieces. Put the pieces into a large bowl.

2. Cut the ends off the cucumber, then slice it finely. Cut the tomatoes in half, then add the cucumber and tomatoes to the bowl.

3. Peel the carrots and cut off their ends. Cut them in half lengthways, then cut them into very thin strips. Add the carrot to the bowl.

4. For the dressing, put the sunflower oil, lemon juice, honey, salt and pepper into a jar with a screw top. Then, screw on the lid.

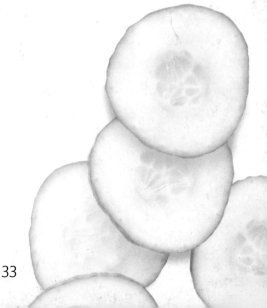

5. Shake the jar to mix the dressing. Pour the dressing over the salad, then gently mix everything together with a spoon and a fork.

Iced daisy biscuits

To make about 30 biscuits, you will need:

75g (3oz) icing sugar

150g (5oz) butter, softened

a lemon

225g (8oz) plain flour

writing icing

small sweets, for decorating

a flower-shaped cookie cutter

2 baking trays, lined with baking
  parchment

Heat your oven to 180°C,
350°F, gas mark 4 in step 6.

✿ Store in an airtight container
and eat within 3 days.

Sift the icing sugar through a sieve.

Use a lemon squeezer.

1. Sift the icing sugar into a large bowl, then add the butter. Stir everything hard with a spoon, until the mixture is creamy.

2. Grate the rind from the lemon using the medium holes on a grater. Then, add the rind to the bowl and mix everything well.

3. Cut the lemon in half and squeeze the juice from it. Then, stir a tablespoon of the juice into the creamy mixture.

Sprinkle some flour on a rolling pin, too.

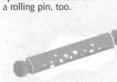

4. Sift the flour into the bowl and mix it in until you have made a smooth dough. Wrap the dough in plastic foodwrap.

5. Put the dough into a fridge for 30 minutes to go firm. Then, sprinkle some flour onto a clean work surface.

6. Turn on your oven. Roll out the dough, until it is about 5mm (¼in) thick. Cut out flower shapes with the cutter.

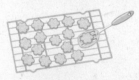

7. Put the flower shapes onto the baking trays. Squeeze the scraps into a ball, then roll it out again and cut out more shapes.

8. Bake the biscuits for 15 minutes. Leave them on the baking trays for 2 minutes. Lift them onto a wire rack to cool.

9. When the biscuits are cool, decorate them with lines, swirls and dots of writing icing. Press sweets onto some of them.

Cherry cake

To make about 8 slices of cake, you will need:
150g (5oz) glacé cherries
200g (7oz) self-raising flour
175g (6oz) caster sugar
175g (6oz) soft margarine
50g (2oz) ground almonds*
3 eggs
a 20 x 12 x 8cm (8 x 5 x 3½in) loaf tin

Heat your oven to 180°C, 350°F,
gas mark 4 in step 3.

✿ Store the cake in an airtight container and eat it within 4 days.

*Don't give this cake to anyone who is allergic to nuts.

1. Cut the cherries into quarters. Rinse them in a sieve under warm running water, then dry them with paper towels.

2. Put the tin onto some baking parchment or greaseproof paper. Draw around the bottom, then cut out the shape.

3. Using some margarine on a paper towel, grease the inside of the tin. Put the paper shape into the tin. Turn on your oven.

4. Sift the flour into a bowl, then add the sugar, margarine and almonds. Break the eggs into a cup, then pour them in, too.

5. Stir the mixture hard with a wooden spoon, until it is light and fluffy. Gently stir in the cherries with a metal spoon.

6. Spoon the mixture out of the bowl into the tin. Then, smooth the top with the back of the spoon, to make it level.

7. Bake the cake for about 1¼ hours, until it has risen. Leave it for 5 minutes, then turn it out onto a wire rack.

8. When the cake is cold, put it onto a chopping board. Then, carefully cut it into about eight slices with a bread knife.

Sunshine toast

To make 1 piece of sunshine toast,
you will need:
margarine
1 slice of wholemeal bread
1 small or medium egg
a large cookie cutter
a baking sheet

Heat your oven to
200°C, 400°F,
gas mark 6,
before you start.

✿ Eat straight away,
while it is hot.

You can use any cutter
that makes a hole that is big
enough to pour an egg into.

38

1. Dip a paper towel into some margarine. Then, use the paper towel to wipe margarine all over the baking tray to grease it.

2. Using a knife, spread margarine on one side of the slice of bread. Then, press the cutter into the middle of the bread to make a hole.

3. Lift out the shape you have cut out. Then, put both pieces of bread onto the baking tray, with the margarine facing up.

4. Crack the egg on the edge of a saucer. Break it onto the saucer, then slide it into the hole in the bread. Put the baking tray into the oven.

5. Bake the sunshine toast in the oven for 7 minutes. Cook it for a little longer if you prefer your egg yolks to be firm rather than runny.

6. Wearing oven gloves, carefully lift the baking tray out of the oven. Then, use a spatula to slide both pieces of toast onto a plate.

Chocolate truffles

To make about 10 truffles, you will need:
100g (4oz) milk chocolate drops
25g (1oz) butter
25g (1oz) icing sugar
50g (2oz) plain cake, crumbled into
    fine crumbs
4 tablespoons of chocolate sugar strands
small paper cases

✿ Store the truffles in an airtight container in
a fridge and eat them within 5 days.

40

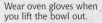
Wear oven gloves when you lift the bowl out.

1. Fill a saucepan a quarter full of water and heat it until the water bubbles. Then, remove the pan from the heat.

2. Put the chocolate drops and butter into a heatproof bowl. Wearing oven gloves, gently put the bowl into the pan.

3. Stir the chocolate and butter with a wooden spoon until they have melted. Carefully lift the bowl out of the water.

4. Using a sieve, sift the icing sugar into the bowl. Add the cake crumbs and stir everything well, to make a smooth mixture.

5. Leave the chocolate mixture to cool in the bowl. While it cools, spread out the chocolate sugar strands on a plate.

6. When the mixture is firm and thick, scoop up some with a teaspoon, then put it into the chocolate strands.

7. Using your fingers, roll the truffle around to make a ball. Carry on until it is covered with sugar strands.

8. Put the truffle into a paper case. Then, make lots more truffles in the same way. Put them all onto a plate.

9. Put the plate into a fridge for 30 minutes to chill the truffles. Store them in an airtight container in the fridge.

Iced sponge cake

To make about 8 slices of cake,
you will need:
225g (8oz) self-raising flour
1 teaspoon of baking powder
225g (8oz) caster sugar
225g (8oz) soft margarine
4 medium eggs
two 20cm (8in) round cake tins

For the butter icing:
225g (8oz) icing sugar
100g (4oz) unsalted butter, softened
1 tablespoon of milk
1 teaspoon of vanilla essence
1 teaspoon of yellow food colouring

Heat your oven to 180°C, 350°F,
gas mark 4, before you start.

✿ Store in an airtight
container in a fridge and
eat within 3 days.

Decorate the cake
with sweets and
marzipan chicks.

1. Put the cake tins onto a piece of greaseproof paper and draw around them. Cut out the circles, just inside the line.

2. Wipe a paper towel in cooking oil and grease the insides of the tins. Lay the paper circles in the tins and grease them, too.

3. Put the flour and baking powder into a sieve over a large bowl. Sift them into the bowl, then add the sugar and margarine.

Use a wooden spoon.

If the middle is springy, the cake is cooked.

4. Break the eggs into a mug, then add them to the bowl. Stir everything well, until you have made a smooth mixture.

5. Spoon half of the mixture into each tin and smooth the tops with the back of the spoon. Bake the cakes for 25 minutes.

6. Press the hot cakes with a finger, to see if they are cooked. Let them cool a little, then put them onto a wire rack.

7. Peel the paper off the cakes, then leave them to cool completely. When they are cold, sift the icing sugar into a bowl.

8. Add the butter, milk, vanilla and colouring. Stir everything hard, until the mixture is fluffy. Then, put one cake onto a plate.

9. Spread the top of the cake with half of the icing. Lay the other cake on top and spread it with the rest of the icing.

Easy pizza

To make 2 pizzas,
you will need:
1 onion
2 cloves of garlic
2 tablespoons of olive oil
400g (14oz) can of chopped
tomatoes
half a teaspoon of dried
mixed herbs
a pinch of salt and of ground
black pepper
1 ciabatta bread
250g (9oz) mozzarella cheese
pizza toppings, such as:
ham, olives, pepperoni,
salami, little tomatoes
2 tablespoons of grated
Parmesan cheese
a large baking tray

Heat your oven to 200°C,
400°F, gas mark 6 in step 5.

❀ Eat the pizzas straight away.

Use a garlic crusher.

Stir the onion and garlic as they cook.

1. Cut off the ends of the onion. Peel off the skin, then cut the onion in half and slice it. Peel the garlic cloves, then crush them.

2. Put the oil, onion and garlic into a frying pan. Gently cook them on a low heat for 5 minutes, or until they are soft.

3. Add the chopped tomatoes, herbs, salt and pepper and stir them in. Turn up the heat and cook the mixture until it boils.

Keep stirring the mixture, to stop it from sticking.

Use a bread knife.

4. Turn the heat down to medium. Then, cook the mixture for about 10 minutes, or until most of the liquid has gone.

5. Take the pan off the heat and leave the mixture to cool for 10-15 minutes. Meanwhile, turn on your oven.

6. Put the bread onto a chopping board and cut it in half along its length. Put both halves onto a large baking tray.

7. Spread each piece of bread with the tomato mixture. Thinly slice the mozzarella cheese, then lay the slices on top.

8. Add any toppings that you want, then sprinkle grated Parmesan cheese on top. Bake the pizzas for about 15 minutes.

9. Lift the pizzas out of the oven and let them cool for 5 minutes. Cut them into pieces and eat them straight away.

Sparkly star biscuits

To make about 20 biscuits, you will need:
3 tablespoons of caster sugar
4 drops of pink food dye
75g (3oz) butter, softened
1 small lemon
3 tablespoons of clear honey
25g (1oz) soft light brown sugar
1 medium egg
175g (6oz) plain flour
plastic foodwrap
medium and small star cookie cutters
two baking trays, wiped with cooking oil

Heat your oven to 180ºC, 350ºF,
gas mark 4, in step 6.

❀ The biscuits need
to be stored in an
airtight container and
eaten within five days.

Stir until the sugar turns pink.

Use the fine holes on the grater.

Use a wooden spoon.

1. Put the caster sugar in a bowl and stir in the food dye. Spread the sugar on a plate to dry. Put the butter in another bowl.

2. Stir the butter until it is creamy. Grate the skin from the lemon. Add the honey, grated lemon and brown sugar to the butter.

3. Stir it until the mixture is smooth. Carefully break the egg on the edge of a small bowl and pour it onto a saucer.

Keep the egg white for later.

4. Put an egg cup over the yolk and dribble the egg white into the small bowl. Stir the yolk into the honey mixture.

5. Sift the flour through a sieve into the mixture and stir. Squeeze the mixture to make a dough. Wrap it in plastic foodwrap.

6. Chill the dough in a fridge for 30 minutes. Dust a rolling pin and clean work surface with flour. Turn on the oven.

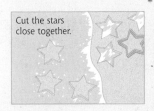

Cut the stars close together.

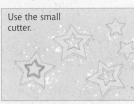

Use the small cutter.

Wear oven gloves.

7. Roll out the dough until it is slightly thinner than your little finger. Cut out stars using the medium cookie cutter.

8. Cut a small star from the middle of each biscuit. Brush some egg white over the stars. Sprinkle them with the pink sugar.

9. Use a spatula to lift the stars onto the oiled baking trays. Bake them for 8-10 minutes. Cool the stars on a wire rack.

Chocolatey bananas

To make 4 baked bananas, you will need:
25g (1oz) butter, softened
40g (1½oz) soft light brown sugar
1 teaspoon of golden syrup
a small pinch of ground cinnamon
4 large, firm bananas
1 tablespoon fresh lemon juice

For the chocolate sauce:
100g (4oz.) plain chocolate drops
2 tablespoons of golden syrup
15g (½oz) butter
2 tablespoons of water

Heat your oven to 200°C, 400°F,
gas mark 6, before you start.

🍀 Eat the
baked bananas
right away.

Use a wooden spoon.

Place the
bananas
lengthways.

1. Cut four 30 x 20cm (12 x 8in) rectangles of kitchen foil for the parcels that the bananas will be baked in.

2. Put the butter into a bowl. Stir it firmly until it is soft and creamy. Then, stir in the sugar, syrup and cinnamon, too.

3. Peel the bananas. Cut them in half lengthways. Rub lemon juice all over them. Lay half a banana on each piece of foil.

4. Spoon the butter and cinnamon mixture onto the flat sides of the half bananas. Press the other halves on top, like this.

5. Fold the ends of the foil over the banana. Pull the sides together over the top, then squeeze them tight to make a parcel.

6. Put the parcels onto a baking tray. Bake them for 15 minutes, until the bananas are soft. As they cook, make the sauce.

Stir the sauce all the time.

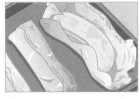

7. Heat the chocolate, syrup, butter and water in a saucepan on a low heat, until you make a smooth sauce. Take it off the heat.

8. Take the parcels out of the oven. Let them cool for about 5 minutes. Open them carefully, and avoid any hot steam.

9. Carefully tip the parcels to slide the bananas and buttery sauce into bowls. Spoon hot chocolate sauce over the top.

Oven-baked omelette

To make an omelette for 4 people, you will need:

1 onion
2 medium-sized potatoes
1 courgette
1 clove of garlic
2 tablespoons of olive oil
15g (½oz) butter
5 medium eggs

150ml (¼ pint) milk
half a teaspoon of mixed herbs
a pinch of salt and of ground black pepper
a shallow 20-23cm (8-9in) ovenproof dish

Heat your oven to 180°C, 350°F, gas mark 4, before you start.

✿ Eat straight away, or allow to cool, then store in a fridge and eat within 2-3 days.

Cut it in half lengthways.

1. To grease the dish, wipe a paper towel in a little butter. Then, wipe butter all over the inside of the dish.

2. Peel the onion. Cut it in half, then slice it finely. Peel the potatoes and cut them in half. Slice them thinly, then chop them.

3. Cut the ends off the courgette. Cut in half, then into strips. Cut the strips into small pieces. Then, peel the clove of garlic.

Use a non-stick frying pan.

Stir the vegetables all the time.

Spread them out evenly.

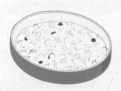

4. Heat the oil and butter on a low heat, until the butter melts. Then, add the onion and potatoes. Cook them for 5 minutes.

5. Add the courgette and crush the garlic into the pan. Gently heat the pan for 5 minutes more, to soften the vegetables.

6. Take the pan off the heat and spoon all the vegetables into the dish. Then, break the eggs into a large bowl.

Lift out the pieces with a spatula or pie slice.

7. Mix the eggs with a fork, then add the milk, herbs, salt and pepper. Then, stir everything together really well.

8. Pour the egg mixture over the vegetables. Then, bake the omelette for 40 minutes, until it is set and golden brown.

9. Push a knife into the middle of the omelette. If runny egg comes out, cook it for 5-10 minutes more. Cut it into pieces.

Tiny iced cakes

To make about 24 little cakes,
you will need:
50g (2oz) self-raising flour
1 medium egg
40g (1½oz) caster sugar
40g (1½oz) soft margarine
small paper cases

For the icing:
50g (2oz) icing sugar
about 1 tablespoon of warm water
2 drops of pink food colouring
writing icing, little sweets and
   sugar sprinkles, for decorating

Heat your oven to 180°C, 350°F,
gas mark 4, before you start.

❀ Store in an airtight container
and eat within 4 days.

Use a wooden spoon.

1. Sift the flour into a large bowl. Break the egg into a mug, then add it to the bowl. Add the caster sugar and margarine, too.

2. Stir everything well, until the mixture is smooth and creamy. Then, put 24 paper cases onto a baking tray.

3. Using a teaspoon, spoon the cake mixture into the paper cases until each case is just under half full, like this.

The cakes will turn golden brown.

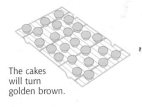

4. Bake the cakes for about 12 minutes, then carefully lift them out of the oven. Put them onto a wire rack to cool.

5. For the icing, sift the icing sugar into a bowl. Add the water and mix it in with a metal spoon until the icing is smooth.

6. To make the icing pink, add the pink food colouring to the bowl. Then, mix it in well with a metal spoon.

7. Spoon a little icing onto the top of each cake with a teaspoon. Then, spread out the icing with the back of the spoon.

8. Leave the icing for a little while to set. Then, decorate the cakes with writing icing. Press on some little sweets, too.

Strawberry trifle

To make a trifle for
4 people, you will need:
500g (1lb) fresh strawberries
6 trifle sponges
2 tablespoons of strawberry jam
4 tablespoons of apple juice
1 small lemon
300ml (½ pint) double cream
2 tablespoons of milk
half a teaspoon of vanilla essence
2 tablespoons of caster sugar

🌸 Cover the trifle with plastic foodwrap,
store it in a fridge and eat it within 2 days.

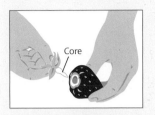

Core

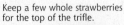
Keep a few whole strawberries for the top of the trifle.

1. Pull the stalks out of the strawberries, trying to keep the core attached. If you need to, dig it out with a small knife.

2. Cut most of the strawberries in half, or into quarters if they are very big. Put them into a medium-sized bowl.

3. Cut the sponges in half and spread them with jam. Press them back together, then cut them into quarters.

4. Lay the sponges on top of the strawberries. Gently mix everything together, then trickle the apple juice over the top.

5. Cover the bowl with plastic foodwrap and put it into a fridge for about 3 hours. The sponges will go soft.

6. Grate the yellow rind from the lemon, using the medium holes on a grater. Scrape off the grated rind with a knife.

Decorate the top with the whole strawberries.

7. When the sponge mixture is cool, pour the cream into a large bowl. Add the milk, lemon rind, vanilla and sugar.

8. Whisk the mixture with a whisk, until it is slightly stiff. Stop before it becomes too solid, or it will be hard to spread.

9. Spread the creamy mixture over the sponge mixture. Then, put the trifle into a fridge until you are ready to serve it.

Chocolate cherry cookies

Makes 24 cookies

75g (3oz) butter, softened
75g (3oz) caster sugar
75g (3oz) soft light brown sugar
1 medium egg
1 teaspoon vanilla essence
175g (6oz) plain flour
½ teaspoon baking powder
50g (2oz) dried cherries
100g (4oz) milk or plain chocolate drops

 These will keep in an airtight
container for 3-4 days.

1. Heat the oven to 180°C, 350°F, gas mark 4. Wipe a little oil over two baking trays. Put the butter and both sugars in a large bowl.

2. Stir the butter and sugar with a wooden spoon until the mixture is smooth and creamy. Break the egg into a small bowl.

3. Beat the egg with a fork, then stir in the vanilla essence. Add the eggy mixture to the large bowl, a little at a time.

Make sure the cookies are well spaced out on the baking trays.

4. Sift the flour and baking powder into the bowl. Stir the mixture until it is smooth. Cut the cherries in half and add them.

5. Add 50g (2oz) of the chocolate drops to the mixture and stir them in. Put a heaped teaspoon of the mixture onto one tray.

6. Use the rest of the mixture to make more cookies. Flatten each one with the back of a fork. Sprinkle on more chocolate.

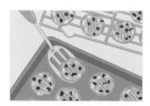

7. Bake the cookies for 10 minutes. Leave them on the trays for a few minutes. Use a spatula to lift them onto a wire rack to cool.

Vegetable goulash

To make a goulash for 4 people, you will need:

1 onion
2 medium-sized potatoes
2 carrots
half a medium-sized cauliflower
1 tablespoon of vegetable oil
1 clove of garlic, crushed
2 teaspoons of paprika
2 tablespoons of plain flour
1 vegetable stock cube
400g (14oz) can of chopped
   tomatoes with basil or
   mixed herbs
a pinch of salt and of ground
   black pepper

❁ Eat straight away, while it is hot.

Ladle the goulash into bowls. Add a spoonful of low-fat soured cream or natural yogurt, a sprinkling of paprika and a parsley leaf.

1. Peel the onion, slice it, then chop it. Peel the potatoes and cut them in half. Slice them, then cut them into little cubes.

2. Peel the carrots and cut them in half. Cut them lengthways, then cut them into pieces about 2.5cm (1in) long.

3. Pull any leaves off the cauliflower. Cut the curly florets off the tough stalk, one at a time. Throw away the leaves and stalk.

Stir them as they cook.

4. Put the vegetable oil, onion and garlic into a large saucepan. Then, gently heat them on a low heat for 5 minutes.

5. When the onions are soft, sprinkle them with the paprika. Sprinkle the flour over them, too, then stir everything well.

6. Put the stock cube into a heatproof jug and add 600ml (1 pint) of boiling water. Stir it until the stock cube dissolves.

Stir everything well.

Stir the goulash every now and then.

7. Pour the stock into the pan. Add the potatoes, carrots, cauliflower florets, chopped tomatoes, salt and pepper, too.

8. Turn up the heat. Heat the goulash until it starts to boil, then reduce the heat, so that it is bubbling gently.

9. Put a lid onto the pan. Gently cook the goulash for about 20-25 minutes, or until the vegetables are cooked.

Apple flapjack

Makes 12 flapjacks

2 eating apples
175g (6oz) butter
175g (6oz) demerara sugar
2 tablespoons golden syrup
½ teaspoon ground cinnamon
50g (2oz) sultanas
225g (8oz) porridge oats
2 tablespoons sunflower seeds
  (optional)
an 18 x 27cm (7 x 11in) tin

❀ These will keep in an
airtight container in the
fridge for 3-4 days.

Draw around
the tin, then cut
along the line.

1. Heat the oven to 160°C, 325°F, gas mark 3. Put the tin on some baking parchment and use a pencil to draw around it. Cut out the rectangle.

2. Grease the tin and lay the parchment inside. Cut the apples into quarters. Peel them, then cut out the cores. Cut the quarters into small chunks.

Use a wooden spoon to stir the mixture every now and then.

3. Put the chunks of apple in a pan with 25g (1oz) of the butter. Cook them over a low heat for ten minutes until the apple is soft.

4. Add the rest of the butter, sugar, syrup, cinnamon and sultanas. Heat them until the butter has melted. Take the pan off the heat.

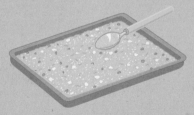

5. Stir in the oats, and the seeds if you are using them. Stir the mixture and spoon it into the tin. Spread it out with the back of a spoon.

6. Put the tin on the middle shelf of the oven. Bake it for 25 minutes. Take it out and leave it to cool for ten minutes. Cut it into pieces.

Strawberry tarts

Makes 12 tarts

For the pastry:
175g (6oz) plain flour
25g (1oz) icing sugar
100g (4oz) chilled butter
1 medium egg
2 teaspoons cold water

For the filling:
300g (10oz) small strawberries
3 tablespoons lemon curd (see
   steps 4-6 in the 'Lemon layer
   cake' recipe to see how to make
   your own)
100ml (4fl oz) double cream

For the glaze:
4 tablespoons redcurrant jelly

a 7½cm (3in) round cutter
a 12-hole shallow bun tray

❀ The cooled pastry cases will keep in
an airtight container for up to 2 days.
Once filled, eat on the same day.

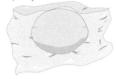

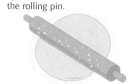

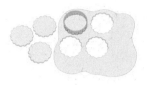

1. Follow steps 1-7 in the 'Sweet pastry' recipe to make the pastry. Heat the oven to 200°C, 400°F, gas mark 6.

2. Put the pastry on a floury surface. Roll out the pastry until it is about 30cm (12in) across and 3mm (⅛ in) thick.

3. Cut circles from the pastry with the cutter. Roll out the leftover pastry and cut more circles. Put a circle in each hole in the tray.

Put the strawberries on a chopping board to cut them.

4. Use a fork to prick each pastry case. Bake them for 10-12 minutes. Then, take them out of the oven and leave them to cool.

5. Rinse the strawberries under cold water. Put them on some kitchen paper to dry. Trim the green stalks with a knife.

6. Spoon the lemon curd into a bowl. Stir in one tablespoon of cream. Pour the rest of the cream into another bowl and whisk it.

Use a teaspoon to spoon the filling into each pastry case.

Make sure the cut sides face down.

Let the glaze cool a little before you brush it over the tarts.

7. Mix together the lemony mixture and the whipped cream. Place the pastry cases on a wire rack. Add some filling to each case.

8. Put a whole strawberry in the middle of each tart. Cut the rest of them in half and place them around the whole strawberry.

9. Heat a pan of redcurrant jelly and two teaspoons of water until the jelly has melted. Brush the glaze over the tarts.

Almond heart sweets

To make about 30 sweets, you will need:
50g (2oz) icing sugar
50g (2oz) caster sugar
100g (4oz) ground almonds*
100g (4oz) full-fat sweetened
  condensed milk
2 drops of red food colouring
one small and one very small
  heart-shaped cutter
a baking tray, lined with
  baking parchment

✿ Store in an airtight container
and eat within 4 days.

*Don't give these to anyone
who is allergic to nuts.

1. Sift the icing sugar into a large bowl. Add the caster sugar and ground almonds, then stir everything together.

2. Make a hollow in the mixture, then pour the condensed milk into it. Stir everything well, until the mixture is smooth.

3. Put half of the mixture into another bowl. Add the red food colouring, then mix it in well with your fingers.

Cut the shapes close together.

4. Wrap both pieces in plastic foodwrap. Then, chill them in a fridge for 20 minutes to make them easier to roll out.

5. Sprinkle a little icing sugar onto a clean work surface. Roll out the pink mixture, until it is about 5mm (¼in) thick.

6. Using the large cutter, cut out lots of heart shapes. Squeeze the scraps into a ball, then roll out the ball.

7. Cut out more hearts. Then, cut holes in the middles of the big hearts with the small cutter. Keep all the shapes.

8. Repeat steps 5-7 with the cream mixture. Then, gently press the small cream hearts into the big pink ones.

9. Press small pink hearts into the big cream ones. Put all the hearts onto the baking tray and leave them to harden overnight.

Couscous salad

To make a salad for 4 people,
you will need:
8 spring onions
1 tablespoon of sunflower oil
half a vegetable stock cube, mixed
    with 225ml (8fl oz) of
    boiling water
225g (8oz) couscous
4 ripe tomatoes

half a cucumber
1 yellow pepper
4 tablespoons of chopped mint

For the dressing:
2 tablespoons of sunflower oil
2 tablespoons of fresh lemon juice
a pinch of salt and of ground
    black pepper

✿ Eat on the day you make it. Serve with
some mixed salad leaves or on its own.

Couscous salad is delicious served with
grilled or barbecued meat or fish, too.

Use a sharp knife.

1. Cut off the ends of the spring onions. Remove the outer layer, then cut the onions into 1cm (½in) diagonal slices.

Use a medium heat.

2. Put the oil and onions into a large saucepan and heat them for 30 seconds. Add the stock, then heat it until the liquid boils.

Use a wooden spoon.

3. Take the pan off the heat. Add the couscous and stir it in. Cover the pan with a lid and leave it for 3 minutes.

Stir the couscous all the time.

4. If there is still any liquid in the pan, gently heat it on a low heat for a few minutes until all of the liquid is absorbed.

5. For the dressing, put the oil into a small bowl. Add the lemon juice, salt and pepper and mix everything with a fork.

Use a fork to break up any lumps.

6. Spoon the couscous into a large bowl. While it is still warm, pour the dressing over it. Stir the couscous, then let it cool.

Throw away the seeds and core.

7. Cut the tomatoes into quarters. Scoop out the seeds with a teaspoon, then cut out the core. Chop the tomatoes finely.

Use a teaspoon.

8. Cut the ends off the cucumber. Cut it in half lengthways. Scoop out the seeds, then chop each half into small pieces.

9. Cut the ends off the pepper and remove the seeds. Chop it finely. Mix the mint and vegetables into the couscous.

Butterfly cakes

To make 8 cakes, you will need:
50g (2oz) self-raising flour
quarter of a teaspoon of
baking powder
1 medium egg
50g (2oz) caster sugar
50g (2oz) soft margarine
paper cake cases
a baking tray with 12 shallow holes

For decorating:
40g (1½oz) butter, softened
2-3 drops of vanilla essence
75g (3oz) icing sugar
about 4 teaspoons of seedless
raspberry jam
extra icing sugar, for dusting

Heat your oven to 190°C, 375°F,
gas mark 5, before you start.

❋ Eat on the day you make them.

1. Sift the flour and baking powder into a large bowl. Break the egg into a mug, then add the egg to the bowl.

2. Add the sugar and margarine. Stir everything with a wooden spoon until you have made a smooth, creamy mixture.

3. Put eight paper cases into the holes in the baking tray. Then, use a teaspoon to half fill each case with the mixture.

Wear oven gloves.

Use a wooden spoon.

4. Bake the cakes for 16-18 minutes, then carefully lift them out of the oven. Put them onto a wire rack to cool.

5. To make the icing, put the butter into a bowl and add the vanilla. Stir them well, until the mixture is really creamy.

6. Sift the icing sugar into another bowl. Add some of the sugar to the butter and stir it in. Repeat this until you have used up the sugar.

Cut the circle a little way in from the edge.

Don't spread the icing all the way to the edge.

7. Using a sharp knife, carefully cut a circle out of the top of each cake. Then, cut each circle in half, across the middle.

8. Spread some icing in the hollow on the top of each cake. Then, spoon half a teaspoon of jam in a line across the icing.

9. Gently push two half circles into the icing on each cake, so that they look like butterfly wings. Sift icing sugar over them.

Lemon ricotta cake

Makes 9 squares

2 lemons
3 eggs
50g (2oz) butter, softened
300g (10oz) caster sugar
250g (9oz) tub ricotta cheese
175g (6oz) self-raising flour
50g (2oz) white chocolate drops
25g (1oz) plain chocolate drops

a 20 cm (8in) square cake tin,
   at least 6½cm (2½in) deep

❀ Store in an airtight container
for up to 4 days.

Save the yolks in a cup.

1. Grease the tin and line it with baking parchment. Heat the oven to 180ºC, 350ºF, gas mark 4. Grate the rind of the lemons.

2. Carefully break one egg on the edge of a cup or bowl. Slide the egg slowly onto a plate. Put an egg cup over the yolk.

3. Holding the egg cup, tip the plate over a bowl, so that the egg white slides into it. Repeat with the other eggs.

4. Whisk the egg whites until they are really thick. When you lift the whisk up, the egg whites should make stiff peaks, like this.

5. Put the butter, sugar, egg yolks and lemon rind into a clean bowl and beat them. Add a spoonful of ricotta and beat again.

6. Add more ricotta until it is all mixed in. Sift in the flour, then fold the mixture with a metal spoon. Fold in the egg whites.

7. Spoon the mixture into the cake tin and smooth it with the back of the spoon. Bake it in the oven for 45-50 minutes.

8. While the cake is still hot, sprinkle the white chocolate drops over the top. Then, scatter the plain chocolate drops.

9. When the drops have melted, use a spoon to swirl the chocolate. Leave the topping to dry, then cut the cakes into squares.

Marshmallow crispies

To make about 12 crispies,
you will need:
100g (4oz) toffee
100g (4oz) butter or margarine
100g (4oz) marshmallows
100g (4oz) rice crispies
a 28 x 18cm (11 x 7in)
shallow tin

❀ Keep in an airtight
container and eat
within 4 days.

They will take about 15 minutes to melt.

1. Dip a paper towel in butter and use it to grease the tin. If you have a slab of toffee, put it in a plastic bag and break it up with a rolling pin.

2. Put the toffee and the butter or margarine into a saucepan. Add the marshmallows. Melt them gently on a low heat, stirring them all the time.

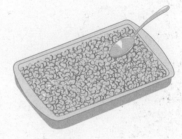

3. When everything has melted and mixed together, carefully take the pan off the heat. Add the rice crispies and gently stir them in.

4. Spoon the mixture into the tin, then press it down gently with the back of a spoon. Leave it to cool and go firm, then cut it into 12 pieces.

Potato and green salads

To make potato salad for 4 people, you will need:

For the potato salad:
675g (1½lb) equal-sized new potatoes
   (cut any bigger potatoes in half)
2 pinches of salt
4 spring onions

For the dressing:
3 tablespoons of mayonnaise
3 tablespoons of Greek or plain
   natural yogurt
1 teaspoon of fresh
   lemon juice
1 teaspoon of
   wholegrain mustard
2 tablespoons of
   chopped fresh dill
a pinch of ground black
   pepper

For the green salad:
2 little gem lettuces,
   or a cos lettuce
1 green pepper
half a cucumber

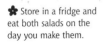 Store in a fridge and
eat both salads on the
day you make them.

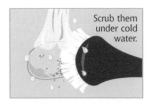

Scrub them under cold water.

1. Scrub the potatoes with a soft brush. Half-fill a large saucepan with water and add the salt. Heat the water until it boils.

2. Add the potatoes. Boil the water, then reduce the heat a little, so that it is gently bubbling. Cook them for 15-20 minutes.

3. Meanwhile, put all of the dressing ingredients into a small bowl. Stir them with a spoon, until they are mixed together.

4. Carefully drain the cooked potatoes through a colander. Shake it gently. Then, leave the potatoes to cool a little.

Use a sharp knife.

5. Cut the ends off the spring onions and peel off the outer layer. Then, cut the onions into lots of thin slices.

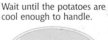

Wait until the potatoes are cool enough to handle.

6. Put the potatoes onto a chopping board and cut them into bite-sized pieces. Put the pieces into a large bowl.

Put the salad in a fridge.

7. Spoon the dressing over the potatoes. Add the slices of spring onion and mix everything well with a large spoon.

Take out the seeds, too.

8. Cut off the bottom of each lettuce. Wash the leaves and shake them dry. Cut the ends off the pepper and slice it finely.

9. Cut the ends off the cucumber. Cut it in half and slice it. Put the slices into a large bowl with the lettuce and green pepper.

Apple crumble

To make a crumble for 6 people,
you will need:
500g (1lb) eating apples
6 tablespoons of water
a large pinch of ground cinnamon
1 tablespoon of caster sugar

For the crumble topping:
100g (4oz) plain flour
100g (4oz) wholemeal flour
100g (4oz) butter
75g (3oz) light soft brown sugar

Heat your oven to 180°C, 350°F,
gas mark 4 in step 2.

✿ Leave the crumble to cool for
5 minutes before you serve it.

Serve the crumble with
cream or ice cream.

1. Cut the apples into quarters. Peel them with a potato peeler, then cut out the cores. Cut the quarters into chunks.

2. Put the apple chunks into a pie dish. Add the water. Sprinkle them with the cinnamon and caster sugar. Turn on your oven.

3. Stir both kinds of flour together in a large bowl. Then, cut the butter into small pieces and add them to the bowl.

4. Stir the butter into the flour with a blunt knife. Keep cutting it and stirring it, until each piece is coated with flour.

5. Wash your hands and dry them well. Then, rub the butter into the flour, lifting the mixture and letting it fall as you rub.

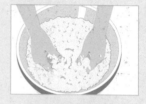

6. Carry on until the mixture looks like coarse breadcrumbs, then add the brown sugar. Mix it in with your fingers.

Smooth the top, too.

7. Spoon the topping over the apple and use a fork to spread it out evenly. Then, put the dish onto a baking tray.

8. Bake the crumble in the oven for 45 minutes, until the top is golden. Then, carefully lift it out, wearing oven gloves.

9. Push a knife into a piece of apple, to see if it is soft. If it isn't soft, cook the crumble for another 5 minutes.

Viennese biscuits

Makes 24 biscuits (12 pairs)

For the biscuits:
175g (6oz) unsalted
butter, softened
40g (1½oz) icing sugar
1 teaspoon vanilla essence
175g (6oz) plain flour
40g (1½oz) cornflour

For the ganache filling:
75g (3oz) plain or milk
chocolate drops
4 tablespoons double cream

✿ Store in an airtight container in
the fridge and eat within 2 days.

Use a wooden spoon to beat the butter and icing sugar together.

1. Heat the oven to 190ºC, 375ºF, gas mark 5. Grease and line two trays. Put the butter in a bowl. Sift over the icing sugar and beat it in.

2. Stir in the vanilla. Sift the flour and cornflour over the top. Stir everything until it is smooth. Put a teaspoon of mixture onto one tray.

3. Put more teaspoons of mixture onto both of the trays, leaving spaces between them. Flatten each blob with the back of a teaspoon.

4. Bake the biscuits for 12-14 minutes. Leave them for five minutes. Use a spatula to lift them onto a wire rack to cool.

5. For the ganache, put the chocolate drops in a heatproof bowl. Add the cream. Then, pour 5cm (2in) water into a pan.

6. Heat the water until it bubbles, then take it off the heat. Carefully, put the bowl in the pan. Stir until the chocolate has melted.

7. Lift the bowl out of the pan and let the ganache cool for a few minutes. Put it in the fridge for an hour, stirring it occasionally.

8. When the ganache is soft like butter, take it out of the fridge. Use a blunt knife to spread some on the flat side of a biscuit.

9. Press another biscuit onto the ganache. Sandwich the biscuits in pairs until all the biscuits and ganache are used up.

Lemon and berry muffins

Makes 12 muffins

1 lemon
250g (9oz) self-raising flour
1 teaspoon bicarbonate
  of soda
150g (5oz) caster sugar
90ml (3½fl oz) sunflower oil
150g (5oz) carton low fat
  lemon-flavoured yogurt
2 medium eggs
150g (5oz) fresh berries
75g (3oz) icing sugar

✿ These are best eaten on the day you make them, but can be stored in an airtight container in the fridge for 2-3 days.

For the lemon icing (optional):
125g (5oz) icing sugar
half a lemon

a 12-hole muffin or deep bun tray
paper muffin cases

You could sift icing sugar over the top to decorate.

1. Put a muffin case into each hole in the tray. Heat the oven to 190°C, 375°F, gas mark 5. Grate the rind of a lemon.

2. Sift the flour and bicarbonate of soda into a bowl and stir in the caster sugar. Make a hollow in the middle of the mixture.

3. Measure the oil into a jug. Add the lemon yogurt and the zest. Juice half the lemon and add the juice to the oily mixture.

4. Break the eggs into a bowl and beat them well. Add them to the oily mixture, then mix the ingredients together.

5. Pour the oily mixture into the hollow in the dry ingredients, then add the berries. Gently stir all the ingredients together.

6. Spoon the mixture into the paper cases. Bake the muffins for 15-18 minutes, then leave them in the tray for five minutes.

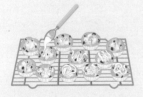

7. Lift the muffins onto a wire rack. To make lemon icing to drizzle on top, mix the juice of half a lemon with the icing sugar.

Ratatouille

To make ratatouille for 4 people,
you will need:
450g (1lb) ripe tomatoes
2 onions
3 courgettes
1 aubergine, weighing about
 350g (12oz)
1 yellow or red pepper
3 tablespoons of olive oil
1 clove of garlic, crushed
half a teaspoon of dried
 oregano or mixed herbs
1 tablespoon of tomato purée
a pinch of salt and of ground black pepper
8 large basil leaves, ripped into small pieces

You could eat the ratatouille with
grilled meat or fish, or spooned
into a jacket potato.

❀ Eat straight away.

The crosses help the skins to peel off.

Cut out the green cores.

1. Cut a cross into the bottom of each tomato. Put them into a heatproof bowl, then fill a second bowl with cold water.

2. Cover the tomatoes with boiling water. After 2 minutes, use a spoon to put them into the cold water for 2 minutes.

3. Lift the tomatoes out, peel them and cut them into quarters. Peel the onions, cut them in half, then chop them finely.

Throw away the ends.

4. Cut the ends off the courgettes, then cut them in half lengthways. Cut them into strips, then cut the strips into chunks.

5. Cut up the aubergine in the same way. Cut the ends off the pepper and remove the seeds. Then, cut it into thin strips.

6. Put the oil and onions into a large saucepan. Cook them on a low heat for about 10 minutes, until the onions are soft.

Keep stirring the ratatouille.

Lift the lid and stir it every now and then.

7. Add the vegetables, garlic, herbs, tomato purée, salt and pepper to the onions in the pan. Stir everything well.

8. Cook the ratatouille on a medium heat for about 3 minutes. Then, turn down the heat, so that it is bubbling gently.

9. Put a lid onto the pan. Cook the ratatouille for 20 minutes, then remove the lid and cook it for 10 minutes. Stir in the basil.

Crunchy peanut cookies

Makes 20 cookies

1 medium egg
100g (4oz) unsalted butter
100g (4oz) soft light brown sugar
100g (4oz) crunchy peanut butter
150g (5oz) self-raising flour
½ teaspoon baking powder
50g (2oz) puffed rice cereal

✿ These will keep in an
airtight container
for 3-4 days.

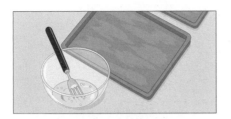

1. Heat the oven to 190ºC, 375ºF, gas mark 5. Grease two baking trays. Break the egg into a small bowl and beat it with a fork.

2. Put the butter and sugar into a bowl. Use a wooden spoon to beat them until they are creamy. Add the egg a little at a time. Beat it after each addition.

3. Add the peanut butter and mix it in really well. Sift the flour and baking powder over the mixture. Then, stir everything together again.

4. Put the puffed rice cereal onto a plate. Scoop up a heaped teaspoon of mixture and shape it into a ball with your hands. Put it on the cereal.

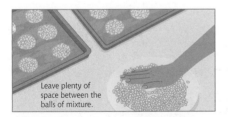

Leave plenty of space between the balls of mixture.

5. Roll the ball in the cereal to cover it. Flatten it very slightly. Put it on a baking tray. Make more balls and place them on the trays.

6. Bake the cookies for 20 minutes. Leave them on the trays for five minutes. Then, use a spatula to lift them onto a wire rack to cool.

Iced muffins

To make 10 muffins, you will need:
2 teaspoons of baking powder
300g (10oz) plain flour
150g (5oz) caster sugar
1 lemon
50g (2oz) butter
225ml (8 fl oz) milk
1 medium egg
100g (4oz) seedless
raspberry jam
small sweets and sugar
strands, for decorating
a 12-hole muffin tin

For the icing:
175g (6oz) icing sugar
2 tablespoons of lemon juice,
squeezed from the lemon
from the main mixture

Heat your oven to 200°C, 400°F,
gas mark 6, before you start.

❀ These muffins are best eaten
on the day you make them.

Use a pastry brush.

Use a lemon squeezer.

1. Brush oil in ten of the holes in the tin. Then, cut a small circle of baking parchment to put into the bottom of each one.

2. Sift the baking powder and flour into a large bowl, then add the sugar. Mix everything together with a metal spoon.

3. Grate the rind from the lemon using the medium holes on a grater. Squeeze the juice from it and keep the juice for the icing.

Heat the pan on a low heat.

4. Cut the butter into small pieces and put them into a saucepan. Then, add the grated lemon rind.

5. Add 4 tablespoons of milk and heat the pan until the butter melts. Take it off the heat and add the rest of the milk.

6. Break the egg into a cup and stir it well with a fork. Then, stir it into the butter mixture and add the mixture to the bowl.

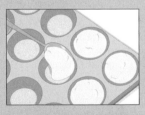

Press on some sweets, too.

7. Stir everything with a fork. Then, nearly fill the ten holes in the tin with the mixture. Bake the muffins for 15 minutes.

8. After 3 minutes, loosen the edges of the muffins, then lift them onto a wire rack to cool. Cut off the top half of each muffin.

9. Spread jam on the bottom halves, then press on the tops. Mix the icing sugar and lemon juice in a bowl. Ice the muffins.

Flower chocolates

To make 12 chocolates, you will need:
75g (3oz) white chocolate drops
3 tablespoons of golden syrup
75g (3oz) plain chocolate drops

❋ Store in an airtight container in a fridge
and eat within a week.

Wear
oven
gloves.

1. Fill a saucepan a
quarter full of water and
heat it until the water
bubbles. Then, remove
the pan from the heat.

2. Put the white
chocolate drops into a
heatproof bowl. Then,
wearing oven gloves, put
the bowl into the pan.

3. Stir the chocolate
until it has melted. Then,
carefully lift the bowl out
of the pan and leave it to
cool for 2 minutes.

Use a wooden
spoon.

4. Stir in 1½ tablespoons
of golden syrup, until
the mixture forms a thick
paste which doesn't stick
to the sides of the bowl.

5. Wrap the chocolate
paste in plastic foodwrap.
Make plain chocolate
paste in the same way,
then wrap it in foodwrap.

6. Chill both pieces of
paste in a fridge for an
hour, then take them out.
Leave them for about 10
minutes, to soften a little.

Wrap one piece and
put it on one side.

Cool the paste in the fridge
again if it gets too soft.

7. Cut the plain chocolate
into seven pieces. Make
six of them into balls.
Squash them a little, then
smooth their edges.

8. Repeat step 7, using
the white chocolate, but
don't wrap any of the
pieces. Then, unwrap the
plain chocolate paste.

9. For the flowers, make
small balls and strips of
chocolate paste. Press a
ball onto each chocolate,
then add petals around it.

Vegetable casserole

To make a casserole for 4 people, you will need:

For the vegetable casserole:
3 medium carrots
4 spring onions
4 button mushrooms
3 cabbage leaves
145g (5oz) tofu
115g (4oz) udon noodles
1 vegetable stock cube
600ml (1 pint) boiling water
2 teaspoons of light soy sauce
2 tablespoons of soft brown sugar
half a teaspoon of salt
a casserole dish with a lid

For the dipping sauce:
2 lemons
6 tablespoons of light soy sauce
1 tablespoon of brown sugar

Heat your oven to 170°C, 325°F, gas mark 3 in step 3.

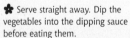 Serve straight away. Dip the vegetables into the dipping sauce before eating them.

1. Peel the carrots and cut off the ends. Cut them in half, then in half lengthways. Cut each piece into thin strips.

2. Trim the ends off the spring onions. Peel off the outer layer. Then, cut the onions into pieces about 2cm (1in) long.

3. Wipe the mushrooms clean. Then, cut the ends off the stems and cut a cross into the top of each one. Turn on your oven.

4. Roll each cabbage leaf into a sausage shape. Slice across each one. The slices will make thin strips when they unroll.

5. Carefully cut the tofu into 2cm (1in) cubes. Then, cook the noodles, following the instructions on the packet.

6. Arrange the vegetables, noodles and tofu in the casserole dish. Then, stir the stock cube and boiling water together in a jug.

Cover the dish with a lid before you put it in the oven.

Use a lemon squeezer.

7. Mix in the soy sauce, brown sugar and salt. Pour the mixture into the dish. Bake the casserole for about 45 minutes.

8. To make the dipping sauce, cut the lemons in half and squeeze them. Put 6 tablespoons of juice into a bowl.

9. Mix the soy sauce and brown sugar into the lemon juice. Chill the dipping sauce in a fridge while the casserole cooks.

Jam tart

To make a large jam tart,
you will need:

350g (12oz) packet of
 shortcrust pastry

plain flour, for dusting

6 rounded tablespoons of seedless
 raspberry or strawberry jam

1 tablespoon of milk

a 20cm (8in) fluted flan tin

a small cutter (any shape you like)

Heat your oven to 200°C, 400°F,
gas mark 6, before you start.

Sift powdered sugar over a slice of jam
tart and serve it with whipped cream.

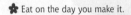 Eat on the day you make it.

1. Take the pastry out of the fridge and leave it for 10 minutes. Then, cut off one quarter and wrap it in plastic foodwrap.

2. Sprinkle a little flour onto a clean surface and a rolling pin. This will help to stop the pastry sticking to them.

3. Roll out the bigger piece of pastry, then turn it a little. Roll it out and turn it, until you make a 30cm (12in) circle.

4. Lay the rolling pin on one side of the pastry. Roll the pastry around it. Lift it up and lay it on the tin, then unroll the pastry.

5. Dip a finger into some flour. Gently press the pastry into the edges of the tin, making sure that you don't rip it.

6. Lay the rolling pin on top of the tin and slowly roll it across, like this. It will cut off the pastry that overlaps the edges.

7. Spoon the jam into the pastry case, then spread it out with the back of the spoon. Roll out the other piece of pastry.

The milk turns the pastry golden brown as it cooks.

8. Using the cutter, cut out about 12 pastry shapes. Brush them with a little milk, then lay them on top of the jam.

Wear oven gloves.

9. Bake the jam tart for about 20 minutes. Then, carefully lift it out of the oven. Let the jam cool before you eat it.

Mini meringues

To make about 15 white and 15 pink meringues,
you will need:
2 eggs, at room temperature
100g (4oz) caster sugar
pink food colouring
2 baking trays, lined with baking parchment

Heat your oven to 110°C, 225°F,
gas mark ¼, before you start.

❀ Store the meringues in an airtight
container and eat them within a week.

If you stick two meringues
together with whipped cream,
eat them straight away.

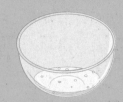

1. Carefully break one of the eggs on the edge of a small bowl, then pour it slowly onto a saucer. Put an egg cup over the yolk.

2. Hold the egg cup over the yolk. Then, gently tip the saucer over the bowl, so that the egg white dribbles into it.

3. Repeat these steps with the other egg, so that the two egg whites are in the bowl. You don't need the yolks in this recipe.

Use a whisk.

4. Whisk the egg whites until they are really thick. They should form stiff points when you lift the whisk up a little.

5. Add a heaped teaspoon of sugar to the bowl. Whisk it in well, then repeat this until you have added all the sugar.

6. Scoop up a teaspoon of the meringue mixture. Use another teaspoon to push it off onto the baking tray, like this.

Let the meringues cool on the baking trays.

7. Make 15 meringues, leaving gaps between them. Then, add 4 drops of food colouring to the rest of the mixture.

8. Gently turn the mixture over with a metal spoon, to mix in the colouring. When it is pink, make 15 more meringues.

9. Bake the meringues for 40 minutes, then turn off the oven. Leave them in the oven for 15 minutes more, then lift them out.

Croque-monsieur

To make 8 pieces of croque-monsieur,
you will need:
8 slices of medium-thick bread
50g (2oz) butter, softened
100g (4oz) Cheddar cheese
4 slices of lean ham
2 teaspoons of sunflower oil

For the mixed salad:
1 little gem lettuce, or
half a cos lettuce
half a cucumber
1 carrot

✿ Eat the croque-monsieurs
straight away, with the
mixed salad.

Sprinkle the
cheese as evenly
as you can.

Use a
sharp knife.

1. Lay four slices of bread on a chopping board. Thinly spread one side of each one with butter, then butter the other four slices.

2. Grate the cheese using the big holes on a grater and sprinkle it over four of the slices of bread. Lay a slice of ham on top.

3. Press a slice of bread onto each one. Cut them in half and put them on a plate. Cover them with plastic foodwrap.

4. Cut the bottom off the lettuce. Rinse the leaves in cold water, then shake them dry. Tear them up and put them into a bowl.

5. Cut the ends off the cucumber. Cut it into four strips, then cut the strips into small chunks. Add them to the bowl.

6. Peel the carrot with a potato peeler. Carefully grate it using the big holes on a grater. Then, add it to the bowl and mix it in.

Use a spatula.

7. Put a teaspoon of the oil into a large, non-stick frying pan. Then, heat it on a medium heat for about a minute.

8. Carefully put four of the pieces into the pan. Cook them for 2-3 minutes, or until their undersides turn brown.

9. Turn the pieces over. Cook them for 2-3 minutes, then lift them out. Add a teaspoon of oil and cook the other four.

Mint choc chip cakes

Try decorating the cakes with
different types of chocolate.

Makes about 25 cakes

40g (1½oz) caster sugar
40g (1½oz) soft margarine
40g (1½oz) self-raising flour
1 tablespoon cocoa powder
1 medium egg
1 tablespoon plain chocolate
   drops
1 tablespoon white chocolate
   drops

❀ Store these in a single layer
in an airtight container for
up to 3 days.

For the peppermint icing:
175g (6oz) icing sugar
1½ tablespoons warm water
1 teaspoon peppermint essence
2 drops green food dye

chocolate drops for decorating

small paper cases

1. Heat the oven to 180°C, 350°F, gas mark 4. Arrange 25 small paper cases on a baking tray. Put the sugar and margarine in a bowl.

2. Sift the flour and cocoa powder into the bowl. Break the egg into a cup, then stir it into the mixture. Divide it into two bowls.

3. Add the plain chocolate drops to one bowl and the white chocolate drops to the other bowl and stir them in with a wooden spoon.

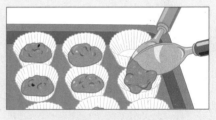

4. Use teaspoons to spoon the mixture into the paper cases. Bake the cakes for 12 minutes, then place them on a wire rack to cool.

5. For the icing, sift the icing sugar into a bowl. Add the warm water, peppermint essence and the green food dye, then stir them in well.

6. Use a teaspoon to spread a little icing onto each cake. Then, decorate the cakes with plain and white chocolate drops.

Crispy apple pies

To make 12 pies, you will need:
100g (4oz) filo pastry (about 6 sheets)
1 medium orange
4 eating apples
50g (2oz) dried cranberries
50g (2oz) caster sugar
half a teaspoon of ground cinnamon
50g (2oz) butter
2 teaspoons of icing sugar
a 12-hole muffin tin or deep
   bun tray

Heat your oven to 190°C, 375°F,
gas mark 5, before you start.

❀ Eat the pies straight away,
while they are warm.

Use the small holes on the grater.

Put a lid on the pan when you're not stirring the mixture.

1. Take the filo pastry out of the fridge, but don't unwrap it. Grate the rind off the orange, then cut the orange in half.

2. Squeeze the juice from the orange. Cut the apple into quarters. Peel them, cut out the cores, then cut the quarters into pieces.

3. Put the apple, rind and 3 tablespoons of juice into a saucepan. Heat the mixture on a low heat for 20 minutes. Stir it often.

The foodwrap will stop the pastry from drying out.

Use a pastry brush.

4. Stir in the cranberries, sugar and cinnamon, then cook the mixture for another 5 minutes. Take the pan off the heat.

5. Unwrap the pastry. Keeping all the sheets together, cut them into six squares. Wrap them with plastic foodwrap.

6. Put the butter into a small pan and melt it on a low heat. Then, brush a little melted butter over one of the pastry squares.

Overlap the pastry sheets, so that they look like a star.

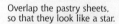

Each case should be nearly full.

7. With the buttered side facing down, gently press the square into a hole in the tin. Add two more buttered squares on top.

8. Fill the other holes. Bake the pastry cases for 10 minutes. Let them cool in the tin for 5 minutes, then take them out.

9. Heat the apple mixture again for 2 minutes, until it bubbles. Spoon it into the cases, then sift icing sugar over the pies.

Cherry crumble cake

Makes 12 slices

For the topping:
75g (3oz) plain flour
25g (1oz) porridge oats
25g (1oz) sunflower seeds
75g (3oz) soft light brown sugar
50g (2oz) butter

For the sponge:
200g (7oz) self-raising flour
1 teaspoon cinnamon
½ teaspoon baking powder
pinch of salt
125g (4½oz) caster sugar
40g (1½oz) butter
2 large eggs
200ml (7fl oz) soured cream
375g (15oz) red cherry jam

a 27 x 18cm (11 x 7in)
rectangular cake tin, at least
4cm (1¾in) deep

✿ Store in an airtight
container for up to 4 days.

1. Heat the oven to 180ºC, 350ºF, gas mark 4. For the topping, sift the flour into a bowl. Add the oats, seeds and sugar.

2. Heat the butter in a saucepan until it melts. Remove the pan from the heat. Pour the butter over the ingredients in the bowl.

3. Use a fork to mix the ingredients in the bowl. Put the bowl into the fridge to chill, while you make the sponge mixture.

4. Sift the cinnamon, flour, baking powder and salt into a bowl. Add the sugar. Melt the butter in a pan, then pour it into a jug.

5. Crack the eggs into a small bowl and beat them. When the butter in the jug is cool, stir in the eggs and the soured cream.

6. Pour the mixture into the dry ingredients. Beat everything until it is smooth. Then, spoon it into a greased, lined tin.

7. Smooth the mixture with a spoon. Put the jam into a bowl and beat it, then use a spoon to drop jam on top of the cake.

8. When the top is almost covered with jam, swirl the jam through the mixture with a knife to make a marbled pattern.

9. Take the topping from the fridge. Break it up and sprinkle it over the cake. Bake the cake for 40 minutes, then let it cool.

Spicy lamb curry

To make a curry for 4 people,
you will need:

1 onion
2 cloves of garlic
3 medium tomatoes
675g (1½lbs) boned lamb
a pinch of salt
4 tablespoons of lemon juice
55g (2oz) butter

1 teaspoon of chilli powder
2 teaspoons of ground coriander
1 teaspoon of ground cumin
1 teaspoon of turmeric
1 teaspoon of ground black pepper
400g (14oz) can of tomatoes
1 meat stock cube
300ml (½ pint) boiling water
300g (11oz) Basmati rice

✿ Eat straight away.

Use a sharp knife.

1. Peel the onion and cut it in half. Slice it and chop it, then peel and crush the garlic. Cut the tomatoes into quarters.

2. Cut the lamb into cubes. Put it into a bowl and mix in the salt and lemon juice. Leave it to soak for 15 minutes.

3. Gently melt the butter in a frying pan. Add the onion and garlic and cook them for about 5 minutes. Soak the rice (see below).

Stir the stock cube until it dissolves.

Stir the curry every now and then.

4. Spoon the lamb into a large saucepan. Then, stir in the spices, pepper, onion, garlic and both kinds of tomatoes.

5. Mix the stock cube with the boiling water, then add it to the pan. Heat the curry on a low heat until it bubbles.

6. Cook the curry for 20-25 minutes. While it cooks, cook the rice (see below), so that everything is ready at the same time.

Cooking the rice

Drain the rice through a large sieve.

1. To soak the rice, fill a bowl with cold water, then add the rice. Leave it for 30 minutes, then drain it through a sieve.

2. Meanwhile, half-fill a pan with water, then heat it until it boils. Add the rice, then bring the water back to the boil.

3. Turn down the heat a little and cook the rice for as long as it says on the packet. Drain it, then rinse it with boiling water.

Raspberry ice cream

To make enough ice cream for 8 people, you will need:
225g (8oz) fresh raspberries
50g (2oz) icing sugar
150ml (¼ pint) Greek yogurt
300ml (½ pint) double or whipping cream
50g (2oz) meringues (bought or home-made)
1 or 2 freezer-proof containers

❀ You need to make the ice cream a day
before you want to eat it. You can store
it in a freezer for up to a week.

Serve the ice cream in
bowls, with a raspberry
and a sprig of mint on top.

Use a fork.

1. Rinse the raspberries in a colander, then dry them on a paper towel. Mash them in a bowl until they are fairly smooth.

2. Using a sieve, sift the icing sugar into the bowl, then stir it in. Add the yogurt to the mixture, then stir everything well.

3. Whisk the cream in another bowl, until it is thick and there are points when you lift the whisk. Add the raspberry mixture.

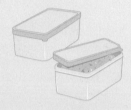

Use a fork.

4. Using a spoon, gently turn the mixture over and over to mix it. Pour it into the containers and put on the lids.

5. Put the ice cream into a freezer for 2 hours, or until it is mushy. While it is in there, break the meringues into pieces.

6. Quickly mash the ice cream to break up any ice crystals. Stir half of the broken meringues into each container.

The ice cream will soften a little.

✿ You shouldn't re-freeze the ice cream when it has been out of the freezer for a while, so put it into two containers if you're not going to eat it all at once.

7. Put the ice cream back into the freezer for 4 hours, or until it is firm. Take it out 15 minutes before you want to eat it.

8. It's easier to serve the ice cream if you use a hot spoon or ice cream scoop. Dip it into a mug of hot water, dry it, then use it.

Coconut truffles

To make about 15 truffles, you will need:
175g (6oz) white chocolate drops
25g (1oz) unsalted butter
50g (2oz) plain sponge cake
4 tablespoons of desiccated coconut
small paper cases

✿ Store the truffles in an airtight container in
a fridge and eat them within 5 days.

1. Fill a large saucepan a quarter full of water and heat it until the water bubbles. Then, remove the pan from the heat.

2. Put the chocolate drops and butter into a heatproof bowl. Wearing oven gloves, carefully put the bowl into the pan.

3. After 2 minutes, stir the chocolate and butter. Keep stirring them until they have melted, then carefully lift out the bowl.

4. Crumble the cake into little crumbs. Add them to the chocolate mixture and stir them in well with a wooden spoon.

5. Spread the coconut on a plate. Scoop up some of the chocolate mixture with a teaspoon, then put it into the coconut.

6. Using your fingers, roll the chocolate mixture in the coconut to make a ball. When it is covered, put it into a paper case.

7. Make more truffles from the rest of the mixture. Put them onto a plate and chill them in a fridge for an hour.

Leek and potato soup

To make soup for 4 people, you will need:
3 leeks
1 onion
40g (1½oz) butter
350g (12oz) potatoes
1 vegetable stock cube
1 bay leaf
a pinch of salt and of ground
   black pepper
300ml (½ pint) semi-skimmed milk

❀ Eat the soup on the day you make it. You can stir a spoonful of low-fat crème fraîche into each bowl and sprinkle with chopped chives, if you like.

Slice the onion before you chop it.

Leave a small gap, to let out the steam.

Use a wooden spoon.

1. Cut the ends off the leeks. Peel off the outer layer, wash them, then slice them. Peel the onion. Cut it in half, then chop it.

2. Heat the butter in a saucepan on a low heat until it melts. Stir in the leeks and onion, then put a lid onto the pan.

3. Cook the onions and leeks for 8-10 minutes, stirring them every now and then. When they are soft, turn off the heat.

4. Peel the potatoes and cut them in half. Slice them, then cut them into chunks. Put the stock cube into a heatproof jug.

5. Add 600ml (1 pint) of boiling water. Stir it until the stock cube dissolves. Add the chunks of potato and the stock to the pan.

6. Add the bay leaf, salt and pepper. Heat the soup until it boils. Reduce the heat, so that it is bubbling gently. Put on the lid.

Press the potatoes with a wooden spoon, to check that they are soft.

7. Cook the soup for 15-20 minutes. Turn off the heat and remove the bay leaf with a spoon. Let the soup cool for 15 minutes.

8. Blend the soup in a food processor, one half at a time. Then, pour the soup back into the pan and stir in the milk.

9. For hot soup, gently re-heat the soup until it is just starting to bubble. For cold soup, put the soup into a fridge to chill.

Choc-chip cookies

To make about 12 cookies, you will need:
100g (4oz) caster sugar
100g (4oz) butter
1 egg
half a teaspoon of vanilla essence
175g (6oz) plain flour
175g (6oz) milk or plain chocolate drops

Heat your oven to 180°C, 350°F,
gas mark 4, before you start.

❀ Keep in an airtight container
and eat within 5 days.

Use a wooden spoon.

1. Wipe a paper towel in a little margarine. Then, grease two baking trays, by wiping the paper towel over them.

2. Put the sugar and butter into a large bowl and stir them well. Carry on stirring until you get a smooth, creamy mixture.

3. Break the egg into a small bowl and mix it well with a fork. Add the vanilla essence to the egg, then mix it in.

Spread out the cookies on both baking trays.

4. Pour the egg into the large bowl and stir it in. Sift the flour through a sieve into the bowl, then stir everything well.

5. When the mixture is smooth, stir in 100g (4oz) of the chocolate drops. You will use the rest of them in step 7.

6. Using a tablespoon, put a heaped spoonful of the mixture onto a baking tray. Then, make 11 more cookies in the same way.

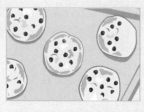

7. Flatten each cookie slightly with the back of a fork. Sprinkle some of the remaining chocolate drops over each one.

8. Bake the cookies for 10-15 minutes. They should be pale golden brown and still slightly soft in the middle.

9. Leave the cookies for a few minutes. Then, use a spatula to lift them onto a wire rack. Leave them to cool completely.

Chocolate raspberry tart

Serves 8

For the pastry:
1 medium orange
175g (6oz) plain flour
25g (1oz) icing sugar
100g (4oz) butter
1 egg

For the filling:
175g (6oz) plain chocolate drops
2 medium eggs
175ml (6fl oz) double cream
75g (3oz) soft light brown sugar
1 tablespoon orange juice

To decorate:
175g (6oz) fresh raspberries
orange rind
1 tablespoon icing sugar
fresh mint

baking beans, or a packet of
   dried beans or peas

a 20cm (8in) flan tin, about
   3½cm (1½in) deep

✿Put on a plate and cover with foodwrap.
Store in the fridge for up to 3 days.

Save the rest of the juice to use in the filling.

1. Grate the rind of the orange. Then, juice the orange. Stir the rind and two teaspoons of the juice in a bowl.

2. Follow steps 1-3 in the 'Sweet pastry' recipe. At step 4, add the rind and juice to the yolk instead of adding water.

3. Follow steps 5-7 in the 'Sweet pastry' recipe. Then, follow the rest of the steps to line the pastry case and bake it 'blind'.

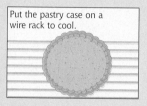

Put the pastry case on a wire rack to cool.

4. Take the pastry out of the oven, then put the tray back in the oven. Reduce the oven temperature to 160°C, 325°F, gas mark 3.

5. For the filling, put the chocolate drops into a heatproof bowl. Heat 5cm (2in) of water in a pan until it bubbles.

6. Take the pan off the heat, then put the bowl in the pan. Stir the chocolate until it melts, then lift the bowl out of the pan.

7. Let the chocolate cool. Break the eggs into a bowl and beat them. Mix in the cream, sugar and one tablespoon of orange juice.

8. Add the chocolate to the mixture a little at a time, stirring between each addition. Then, pour it into the pastry case.

9. Bake the tart for 30 minutes. When it is cool, decorate it with raspberries, orange rind, sifted icing sugar and fresh mint.

Greek salad

To make a salad for 4 people, you will need:
half a cucumber
450g (1lb) ripe tomatoes
1 red onion
200g (7oz) packet of feta cheese
75g (3oz) stoned black or
    green olives, drained

For the dressing:
1 clove of garlic
4 tablespoons of olive oil
1 tablespoon of white wine vinegar
quarter of a teaspoon of dried
    oregano
a pinch of caster sugar
a pinch of salt and of
    ground black pepper

✿ Eat on the day you
make it and serve with
bread rolls.

Core

1. Cut the ends off the cucumber, then cut it in half along its length. Lay each half flat side down, then cut the cucumber into thin slices.

2. Cut the tomatoes into quarters, then cut out the green cores. Then, put the tomato quarters and cucumber slices into a large bowl.

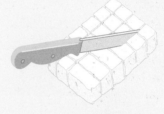

3. Peel the onion. Cut it into quarters, then cut each quarter into slices. Open the packet of feta and pour away any liquid.

4. Cut the feta into cubes, then add it to the bowl. Add the onion and most of the olives, then use your hands to mix everything together.

You need to use a jar with a lid.

5. Peel and crush the garlic. Then, put the oil, vinegar, garlic, oregano, sugar, salt and pepper into a jar. Screw the lid on tightly.

6. Shake the jar well. Drizzle the dressing over the salad and mix it in. Then, scatter the rest of the olives over the top.

117

Choc-chip muffins

To make 12 muffins, you will need:
250g (9oz) self-raising flour
a pinch of salt
1 teaspoon of baking powder
50g (2oz) butter
75g (3oz) soft light brown sugar
100g (4oz) chocolate drops
2 eggs
2 teaspoons of vanilla essence
250ml (8 fl oz) milk
a 12-hole deep bun or muffin tin
12 paper muffin cases

Heat your oven to 200°C, 400°F,
gas mark 6 in step 2.

✿ Eat straight away, or store
in an airtight container and
eat within 3 days.

To make double chocolate
muffins, use 225g (8oz) of
self-raising flour and 25g
(1oz) of cocoa powder.

1. Wipe a paper towel in some margarine, then use it to grease the holes in the tin. Put a paper case into each hole.

2. Sift the self-raising flour, salt and baking powder through a sieve into a large bowl. Then, turn on your oven.

3. Cut the butter into chunks and add it to the flour mixture. Rub in the butter, until the mixture looks like breadcrumbs.

Mix the chocolate drops evenly into the mixture.

4. Add the sugar and about three-quarters of the chocolate drops. Stir them into the mixture with a wooden spoon.

5. Break the eggs into a bowl and stir them hard with a fork. Add the vanilla and milk, then stir everything well.

6. Pour the egg mixture into the flour. Quickly mix everything with a fork. The mixture will still be a little lumpy.

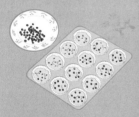

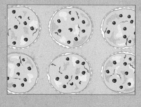

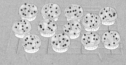

7. Spoon the mixture into the paper cases, filling them almost to the top. Sprinkle the rest of the chocolate drops on top.

8. Bake the muffins in the oven for about 20 minutes, until they have risen in the paper cases and their tops are firm.

9. Leave the muffins in the tin for 5 minutes. Then, eat them straight away, or put them onto a wire rack to cool.

Tiny iced cookies

To make about 100 tiny cookies,
you will need:
50g (2oz) butter, softened
75g (3oz) caster sugar
1 egg yolk
1 teaspoon of clear honey
2 teaspoons of milk
1 teaspoon of vanilla essence
100g (4oz) plain flour
25g (1oz) cornflour
2 greased baking trays
small cutters

For the icing:
150g (5oz) icing sugar
2 tablespoons of warm water
pink food colouring

Heat your oven to 180°C, 350°F,
gas mark 4, before you start.

✿ Store in a single layer in an airtight
container and eat within 3 days.

Use a wooden spoon.

1. Put the butter and sugar into a large bowl. Stir them hard, until they look creamy. Then, add the egg yolk and stir it in.

2. Stir in the honey, milk and vanilla essence. Sift the flour and cornflour into the bowl, then mix everything well.

3. Squeeze the mixture in your hands, until you have made a ball of dough. If it is a little dry, add a drop of milk.

The cookies turn golden brown.

4. Sprinkle flour onto a work surface. Roll out the dough until it is about 5mm (¼in) thick. Use the cutters to cut out shapes.

5. Put the shapes onto the baking trays. Then, squeeze the scraps into a ball, roll it out and cut out more shapes.

6. Bake the shapes for 6-8 minutes, then carefully lift them out of the oven. Leave them on the baking trays to cool.

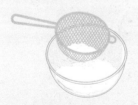

Use a blunt knife.

7. To make the icing, sift the icing sugar into a bowl. Mix in the water, then spoon half of the icing into another bowl.

8. Cover one bowl with plastic foodwrap, to stop the icing drying out. Mix 2 drops of food colouring into the other bowl.

9. Spread half of the tiny cookies with the white icing and half with pink icing. Then, leave the icing to set.

Pasta with tomatoes

To make pasta for 4 people, you will need:

For the sauce:
680g (1½lb) ripe tomatoes
2 cloves of garlic, crushed
1 tablespoon of olive oil
a pinch of caster sugar
half a teaspoon of dried oregano or mixed herbs
a pinch of salt and of ground black pepper
12 basil leaves, ripped into small pieces

For the pasta:
a pinch of salt
1 tablespoon of olive oil
350g (12oz) dried pasta shapes

❀ Eat straight away.

This recipe used a kind of
pasta called farfalle, but
you can use any shape.

The crosses help the skins to peel off.

Make sure your hands are clean.

1. Cut a cross into the bottom of each tomato. Put them into a heatproof bowl, then fill a second bowl with cold water.

2. Cover the tomatoes with boiling water. Leave them in the bowl for 2 minutes, then lift them out with a slotted spoon.

3. Put the tomatoes into the cold water for 2 minutes. Lift them out, peel off their skins, then cut them into quarters.

Use a medium heat.

Leave a small gap, so that the steam can escape.

4. Scoop out the seeds with a teaspoon. Then, carefully cut out the core and cut all the quarters into small pieces.

5. For the sauce, put the tomatoes, garlic, olive oil, sugar, herbs, salt and pepper into a saucepan. Heat it for 2 minutes.

6. Cover the pan with a lid, then turn down the heat. Cook the sauce on a low heat for about 15 minutes, stirring it often.

Cook the pasta while the sauce cooks.

Stir the sauce while the pasta cooks.

7. Half-fill a pan with water. Add a pinch of salt and a tablespoon of olive oil. Boil the water, then add the pasta and stir it.

8. Boil the water again, then reduce the heat, so that it is bubbling gently. Cook the pasta for as long as it says on the packet.

9. Drain the pasta in a colander. Then, stir the ripped basil into the sauce. Spoon the pasta and sauce into bowls.

Cheesy chick biscuits

To make about 15 biscuits, you will need:
75g (3oz) mature Cheddar cheese
100g (4oz) plain flour
50g (2oz) butter, refrigerated
the yolk from a medium egg
5 teaspoons of cold water
a cookie cutter
2 greased baking trays

Heat your oven to 190°C, 375°F,
gas mark 5 in step 5.

❀ Store the chicks in an airtight container
and eat them within 4 days.

Use the small holes on a grater.

1. Grate the cheese. Sift the flour through a sieve into a large bowl. Then, cut the butter into chunks and add it to the bowl.

2. Mix in the butter, then rub it in with your fingers, until the mixture looks like breadcrumbs. Add half of the cheese.

3. Mix the egg yolk and water in a small bowl. Put 2 teaspoonfuls into a cup, then pour the rest over the flour mixture.

4. Stir everything well. Squeeze the mixture until you have made a smooth dough, then make it into a slightly flattened ball.

5. Wrap the dough in plastic foodwrap and put it into a fridge to chill for 30 minutes. While it chills, turn on your oven.

6. Sprinkle flour onto a clean work surface and a rolling pin. Then, roll out the dough, until it is about 5mm (¼in) thick.

Leave spaces between the shapes.

Use the mixture from step 3.

Use a spatula.

7. Cut out shapes with the cookie cutters. Put them onto the baking trays. Squeeze the scraps into a ball, then roll them out.

8. Cut out more shapes. Brush egg mixture over the top of each shape, then sprinkle them with grated cheese.

9. Bake the biscuits for 12 minutes. Leave them on the baking trays for 5 minutes, then lift them onto a wire rack to cool.

🌸 These will keep in an airtight container for 2-3 days.

Chocolate marzipan hearts

Makes 20 hearts

100g (4oz) self-raising flour
25g (1oz) cocoa powder
75g (3oz) chilled butter
50g (2oz) caster sugar
1 medium egg

100g (4oz) marzipan
1 teaspoon icing sugar
½ teaspoon cocoa powder

a medium and a small
    heart-shaped cutter

1. Grease a baking tray. Sift the flour and cocoa powder into a large bowl. Cut the butter into chunks. Add them to the mixture.

2. Coat the butter with flour. Rub it with your fingertips until the mixture looks like breadcrumbs. Stir in the sugar.

3. Break the egg onto a plate. Hold an egg cup over the yolk. Tip the plate, so the white slides into a bowl. Add the yolk to the mixture.

Use the smaller cutter.

4. Stir the mixture into a dough. Use your hands to squeeze it into a ball. Wrap it in foodwrap. Put it in the fridge for 30 minutes.

5. Sprinkle icing sugar onto a clean surface. Roll out the marzipan until it is 3mm (1/8 in) thick. Cut out some small hearts.

6. Squeeze the scraps into a ball. Roll it out and cut out more hearts until you have 12. Heat the oven to 200°C, 400°F, gas mark 6.

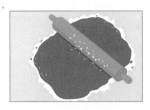

7. Sprinkle flour onto a clean surface. Roll out the dough until it is 3mm (1/8 in) thick. Use the large cutter to cut out 24 hearts.

8. Put half the chocolate hearts on the tray. Put a marzipan heart on each one. Put a second chocolate heart on top.

9. Press the edges together, then bake them for ten minutes. Sift icing sugar over them, then cocoa. Lift them onto a wire rack.

Pasta with vegetables

To make pasta for 4 people, you will need:
4 spring onions
225g (8oz) broccoli
125g (4oz) thin green beans
125g (4oz) mangetout
1 courgette
25g (1oz) butter
375g (12oz) dried or
  400g (14oz) fresh tagliarini
250g (8oz) soft cheese with
  garlic and herbs

❀ Eat straight away.

Use a sharp knife.

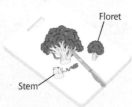
Floret

Stem

1. Cut the ends off the spring onions. Remove the outer layer. Then, cut the onions into pieces about 3cm (1in) long.

2. Cut the tough stem off the broccoli and throw it away. Then, cut off the curly florets and rinse them in a colander.

3. Using clean kitchen scissors, trim the ends off the green beans and mangetout. Then, cut them all in half.

Use a low heat.

4. Cut the ends off the courgette. Cut it in half across the middle. Then, slice each half into thin strips, like this.

5. Half-fill a saucepan with water. Heat it until it boils. Cook the broccoli and beans for 3 minutes, then drain them.

6. Boil a pan of water for the pasta, then turn it off. Gently melt the butter in a frying pan, then add the onions, broccoli and beans.

Stir the vegetables as they cook.

Stir in a little milk if the sauce is too thick.

7. Cook the vegetables for 5 minutes, then add the mangetout and courgette. Cook them all for another 3 minutes.

8. Boil the pan of water again. Cook the pasta for 3 minutes, then drain it. Put it back into the pan and mix in the vegetables.

9. Add the cheese and break it up with a spoon. Then, gently cook the mixture on a low heat until the cheese melts.

Fruit scones

Makes 9 scones

200g (8oz) self-raising
  flour
50g (2oz) caster sugar
50g (2oz) margarine
¼ teaspoon of salt
100g (4oz) sultanas
1 medium egg

75ml (5 tablespoons) milk
6cm or 7cm (2½in)
  round cutter

❁ These are best eaten on the
day you make them, but can be
stored in an airtight container
for up to two days.

1. Heat the oven to 220ºC, 425ºF, gas mark 7. Sift the flour into a large bowl. Add the sugar, margarine and salt.

2. Use your fingertips to rub in the margarine, until the mixture looks like breadcrumbs. Stir in the sultanas.

3. Break the egg into a small bowl and beat it. Stir in the milk. Put one tablespoon of the mixture into a cup to use later.

4. Pour some of the mixture into the large bowl and stir. Repeat until all the mixture is added, to form a dough.

5. Sprinkle a work surface with flour. Roll out the dough until it is 1½cm (½in) thick. Use the cutter to cut out circles.

Leave a space between each scone.

6. Roll out the leftover dough and cut out more circles. Put them all on the tray. Brush them with the eggy mixture.

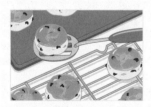

7. Bake the scones in the oven for ten minutes, then carefully take them out. Use a spatula to lift them onto a wire rack to cool.

Pretty fudge shapes

To make about 70 fudge shapes, you will need:
450g (1lb) icing sugar
100g (4oz) pink marshmallows
2 tablespoons of milk
100g (4oz) unsalted butter
half a teaspoon of vanilla essence
red food colouring
small cutters
small sweets, for decorating

✿ Store in an airtight container in a fridge and eat within a week.

1. Sift the icing sugar through a sieve into a large bowl. Make a small hollow in the middle of the sugar with a spoon.

2. Cut the marshmallows in half. Put them into a small saucepan, then add the milk, butter and vanilla essence.

Use clean kitchen scissors.

3. Heat the mixture on a low heat until everything has just melted. Stir it with a wooden spoon every now and then.

4. Pour the mixture into the hollow in the sugar. Add a drop of red food colouring, then stir the mixture until it is smooth.

5. Leave the mixture to cool for 10 minutes. Make it into a flattened round shape, then wrap it in plastic foodwrap.

6. Put the fudge into a fridge for 3 hours to go firm. Then, sprinkle a little icing sugar onto a clean surface.

To make 'white' fudge shapes, use white marshmallows and don't add any food colouring.

7. Using a rolling pin, roll out the fudge until it is about 5mm (¼in) thick. Use the cutters to cut out lots of shapes.

8. Squeeze the scraps into a ball, then roll out the ball and cut out more shapes. Press a sweet onto each shape.

Chilli con carne

To make chilli con carne for
4 people, you will need:
half a beef or vegetable
  stock cube
1 onion
1 clove of garlic, crushed
1½ tablespoons of vegetable oil
450g (1lb) minced beef
2-3 teaspoons of mild chilli powder
1 teaspoon of ground cumin

400g (14oz) can of red kidney beans
400g (14oz) can of chopped
  tomatoes
1 tablespoon of tomato purée
1 teaspoon of soft dark brown sugar
half a teaspoon of dried mixed herbs
2 pinches of salt and of ground
  black pepper

✿ Serve right away, with boiled rice,
noodles or spooned into a baked potato.

Use a large pan.

Stir everything often.

1. Put the stock cube and 225ml (8fl oz) of boiling water into a heatproof jug. Stir them well, then put the jug aside.

2. Peel the onion and cut it in half. Slice it, then cut it into small pieces. Put the onion, garlic and oil into a saucepan.

3. Gently heat the pan on low heat for 10 minutes. Then, turn the heat up to medium and add the minced beef.

Use a colander.

4. Cook the beef for 10 minutes, or until it is brown. Stir it all the time, breaking up any lumps with a wooden spoon.

5. Take the pan off the heat. Stir in the chilli powder and cumin. Open the can of beans and rinse them under cold water.

6. Add the beans, broth, tomatoes, tomato purée, sugar, herbs, salt and pepper to the pan. Then, stir everything well.

The steam escapes through the gap.

7. Heat the chilli con carne until it boils. Stir it, then reduce the heat to low. Put a lid onto the pan, leaving a small gap.

8. Cook the chilli for 15 minutes, then remove the lid. Cook it for 15 minutes more, stirring it every now and then.

Pretty pear tarts

To make 12 pear tarts, you will need:
375g (13oz) shortcrust pastry, taken
  out of the fridge 20 minutes before
  you start.
1 small orange
15g (½oz) butter
25g (1oz) dried cranberries
25g (1oz) soft light brown sugar
half a teaspoon of ground cinnamon
2 soft, sweet pears or 4 pear halves
  from a can
milk, for glazing
a greased 12-hole baking tray
a 7.5cm (3in) round cutter and
  a smaller star-shaped cutter

Heat your oven to 190°C, 375°F,
gas mark 5 in step 5.

Sift a little icing
sugar over the
tarts before you
serve them.

❀ Eat straight away, or store in an
airtight container and eat within 3 days.

You don't need the other half of the orange.

Cut tinned pears into small pieces.

1. Grate half of the rind from the orange using the small holes on a grater. Cut it in half and squeeze the juice from one half.

2. Put the rind and 1 tablespoon of the juice into a saucepan. Add the butter, cranberries, brown sugar and cinnamon.

3. Using a potato peeler, carefully peel the pears. Cut them into quarters and cut out the cores. Cut the quarters into small pieces.

Stir the mixture all the time.

Dust the rolling pin with flour, too.

Cut the circles close together.

4. Put the pieces of pear into the pan. Heat the mixture on a low heat for 10 minutes. Take it off the heat, then let it cool.

5. Turn on your oven. Dust a clean work surface with flour, then roll out the pastry until it is about 5mm (¼in) thick.

6. Cut 12 circles from the pastry with the round cutter. Then, squeeze the scraps to make a ball and put it to one side.

The milk will make the pastry shiny.

Wear oven gloves.

7. Press the circles into the holes in the baking tray. Then, put a heaped teaspoon of the pear mixture into each one.

8. Roll out the ball of pastry. Cut out 12 stars with the star cutter. Lay them on the tarts, then brush them with milk.

9. Bake the tarts for 20 minutes, then lift them out. After 10 minutes, lift them out of the tray with a blunt knife.

Cherry crunches

To make about 15 cherry crunches,
you will need:
25g (1oz) glacé cherries
25g (1oz) rich tea or other plain biscuits
25g (1oz) white marshmallows
100g (4oz) white chocolate drops
25g (1oz) unsalted butter
15 dried cranberries
small paper cases

✿ Store in an airtight
container in a fridge
and eat within a week.

1. Cut the cherries into tiny pieces. Put them into a large bowl. Break the biscuits into little pieces and add them, too.

2. Cut the marshmallows into little pieces, using clean kitchen scissors. Add them to the bowl and mix everything well.

3. Fill a large saucepan a quarter full of water and heat it until the water bubbles. Then, remove the pan from the heat.

4. Put the chocolate drops and butter into a heatproof bowl. Wearing oven gloves, carefully put the bowl into the pan.

5. After 2 minutes, stir the mixture with a metal spoon. When everything has melted, carefully lift the bowl out of the pan.

6. Spoon the chocolate and butter mixture into the large bowl. Then, use a wooden spoon to mix everything well.

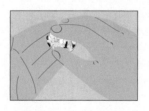

7. Scoop up some of the mixture with a teaspoon. Shape it into a ball with your fingers, then put it into a paper case.

8. Make lots more balls, until you have used up all of the mixture. Then, press a dried cranberry on top of each ball.

9. Put all the crunches onto a large plate. Then, put the plate into a fridge and leave them to chill for 2 hours.

Macaroni cheese

To make macaroni cheese for 4 people, you will need:
175g (6oz) dried macaroni
50g (2oz) butter
50g (2oz) plain flour
600ml (1 pint) milk
a pinch of salt and of ground black pepper
200g (7oz) Cheddar or Gruyère cheese, grated

Heat your oven to 180°C, 350°F, gas mark 4, before you start.

♣ Eat straight away.

Serve with lettuce and slices of cucumber.

Drain the macaroni through a colander.

Use a wooden spoon.

Add the salt and pepper, too.

1. Boil the macaroni following the instructions on the packet. When it is cooked, drain it, then tip it back into the pan.

2. To make the sauce, melt the butter in a saucepan on a low heat. Stir in the flour and cook the mixture for 1 minute.

3. Take the pan off the heat and add a little milk. Stir it in really well, then stir in the rest of the milk, a little at a time.

4. Heat the pan again and start to bring the sauce to the boil. Stir it all the time to stop it sticking to the pan.

5. The sauce will begin to thicken. Let it bubble for 1 minute, then take it off the heat. Stir in 175g (6oz) of the cheese.

6. Pour the sauce over the cooked macaroni. Stir it in really well, so that it coats all of the pieces of macaroni.

7. Dip a paper towel into some margarine and rub it over the inside of an ovenproof dish. Pour in the cheesy macaroni.

8. Sprinkle the rest of the cheese over the top. Bake the macaroni cheese for about 25 minutes, until the top is golden brown.

9. Wearing oven gloves, lift the dish out of the oven. Let the macaroni cheese cool for a few minutes, then serve it.

Cobweb cookies

To make about 18 cookies, you will need:
160g (5½oz) plain flour
2 tablespoons of cocoa powder
100g (4oz) butter, refrigerated
50g (2oz) caster sugar
2 tablespoons of milk
a 6.5cm (2½in) round cutter
2 baking trays, lined with baking parchment
white writing icing
a cocktail stick

Heat your oven to 180°C, 350°F,
gas mark 4 in step 4.

❋ Store the cookies in a single layer
in an airtight container and eat
them within 5 days.

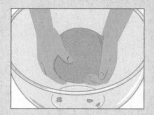

1. Sift the flour and cocoa into a large bowl. Cut the butter into chunks and add it to the bowl. Then, rub it in with your fingers.

2. When the mixture is like fine breadcrumbs, stir in the sugar. Sprinkle the milk over the mixture and stir it in with a fork.

3. Stir the mixture until everything starts to stick together. Then, squeeze it with your hands to make a ball of dough.

Make the dough into a squashed circle.

The flour stops the dough sticking.

Use a spatula.

4. Wrap the dough in plastic foodwrap and put it into a fridge to chill for 20 minutes. Meanwhile, turn on your oven.

5. Sprinkle some flour on a clean work surface and a rolling pin. Then, roll out the dough, until it is about 5mm (¼in) thick.

6. Using the cutter, cut out lots of circles and lift them onto the baking trays. Squeeze the scraps together to make a ball.

Wear oven gloves.

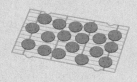

7. Roll out the ball again and cut out more circles. Bake the cookies for 10-12 minutes, then lift them out of the oven.

8. Leave the cookies on the baking trays for 5 minutes. Then, lift them onto a wire rack and let them cool completely.

9. Draw a spiral of icing on a cookie. Use a cocktail stick to drag lines from the middle to make a web. Ice webs on all the cookies.

Carrot cake

To make about 12 slices of cake,
you will need:

For the cake:
2 medium carrots
3 medium eggs
200g (7oz) caster sugar
175ml (6fl oz) sunflower oil
100g (4oz) chopped pecans*
200g (7oz) plain flour
1½ teaspoons of baking powder
1½ teaspoons of bicarbonate
 of soda
1½ teaspoons of ground cinnamon
1 teaspoon of ground ginger
half a teaspoon of salt

a 27 x 18cm (7 x 11in) shallow
 rectangular cake tin

For the topping:
50g (2oz) icing sugar
200g (7oz) full fat cream cheese,
 at room temperature
1 tablespoon of lemon juice
half a teaspoon of vanilla essence
pecans or lemon rind, to decorate

Heat your oven to 180°C, 350°F,
gas mark 4, before you start.

❀ Store in a fridge and eat within 2 days.

*Don't give this cake to anyone
who is allergic to nuts.

Use the big
holes on
the grater.

Use a
wooden
spoon.

1. Dip a paper towel into cooking oil and grease the tin. Then, lay the tin on greaseproof paper and draw around it.

2. Cut out the rectangle and lay it in the tin. Wash the carrots and cut off their ends, then carefully grate them on a grater.

3. Break the eggs into a small bowl. Mix them well with a fork. Put the sugar and oil into a large bowl and stir them for 1 minute.

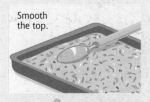

Smooth
the top.

4. Stir the eggs into the sugary mixture, a little at a time. Then, stir in the grated carrots and chopped nuts, too.

5. Sift in the flour, baking powder, bicarbonate of soda, cinnamon, ginger and salt. Gently turn the mixture with a spoon.

6. When the mixture is well mixed, spoon it into the tin. Bake the cake for 45 minutes, until it is well-risen and firm.

Peel off the greaseproof paper.

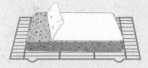

Use a blunt knife.

7. Leave the cake in the tin for 10 minutes. Run a knife around the sides, then turn it out onto a wire rack. Leave it to cool.

8. For the topping, sift the icing sugar into a bowl. Add the cream cheese, lemon juice and vanilla. Stir everything well.

9. Spread the topping over the top of the cake. Cut the cake into squares, then decorate them with pecans or lemon rind.

Coconut chicken curry

To make a curry for 4 people, you will need:

4 skinless, boneless chicken breasts
2 level teaspoons of cornflour
300ml (½ pint) thick plain yogurt
1 onion
2 tablespoons of vegetable oil
2 cloves of garlic, crushed
half a teaspoon of ground ginger
half a teaspoon of ground turmeric

2 teaspoons of ground coriander
1 teaspoon of ground cumin
150ml (¼ pint) coconut milk
1 chicken stock cube, mixed with
  75ml (3fl oz) of boiling water
a pinch of salt and of ground
  black pepper
2 tablespoons of chopped fresh
  coriander

✿ Serve with boiled Basmati rice.

146

1. Trim any white fat off the chicken breasts. Cut each chicken breast into three equal-sized pieces. Wash your hands well.

2. Mix the cornflour and 2 tablespoons of yogurt in a bowl. Then, mix in the rest of the yogurt, a little at a time.

3. Cut the ends off the onion and peel off the skin. Cut the onion in half, slice it, then cut it into small pieces.

4. Put the onion into a large saucepan with the oil. Cook it on a low heat for 10 minutes, then take it off the heat.

5. Add the garlic, ginger, turmeric, coriander and cumin. Gently heat the mixture for 2 minutes, stirring it all the time.

6. Turn the heat down very low and add the chicken. Add and stir in the yogurt mixture, 1 tablespoon at a time.

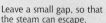

If the chicken is
cooked, it will
be white inside.

7. Stir in the coconut milk and stock, a little at a time. Mix in the salt and pepper, too, then put a lid onto the pan.

8. Cook the curry on a low heat for 30 minutes, stirring it often. Then, cut a piece of chicken in half, to see if it is cooked.

9. If the chicken is even slightly pink, cook it for another 5-10 minutes, then check it again. Stir in the chopped coriander.

Creamy chocolate fudge

To make about 36 squares of fudge, you will need:

½ teaspoon of oil, for wiping
75g (3oz) full-fat cream cheese
350g (12oz) icing sugar
1 level tablespoon of cocoa powder
75g (3oz) plain chocolate drops
40g (1½oz) butter
a shallow 15cm (6in) square cake tin
greaseproof paper

✿ This fudge needs to be
eaten within a week.

Use a pencil to draw around the tin.

1. Put the cake tin onto a sheet of greaseproof paper and draw around it. Cut out the shape, just inside the line.

Use a paper towel.

2. Wipe cooking oil onto the sides and base of the tin. Press the paper square into the base and wipe it too.

3. Put the cream cheese into a bowl. Sift the icing sugar and cocoa through a sieve into the bowl. Mix them together well.

Ask someone to help you with this stage.

4. Melt the chocolate and butter in a heatproof bowl placed in a pan of hot water. Wear oven gloves to lift the bowl.

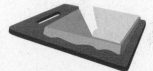

5. Stir a tablespoon of the cream cheese mixture into the chocolate. Then pour the chocolate into the cheese mixture.

6. Beat the chocolate and cheese together until they are creamy. Spoon the mixture into the tin, pushing it to the corners.

Make the top of the fudge as smooth as you can.

7. Smooth the top of the fudge with a spoon. Keep the tin in a fridge for two hours, or until the fudge is firm.

8. Use a blunt knife to loosen the edges of the fudge, then turn it out onto a large plate. Remove the paper.

9. Cut the fudge into lots of small squares. Then, put the plate in the fridge for two hours, until the fudge is hard.

Chocolate fudge brownies

Makes 9 squares

100g (4oz) plain chocolate drops
2 large eggs
½ teaspoon vanilla essence
125g (5oz) butter, softened
275g (10oz) caster sugar
50g (2oz) self-raising flour
25g (1oz) plain flour

2 tablespoons cocoa powder
100g (4oz) walnuts or pecans

a 20cm (8in) square cake tin, at
  least 6½cm (2½in) deep

❀ Store these in an airtight container
in the fridge for up to 4 days.

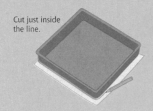

Cut just inside the line.

1. Heat the oven to 180°C, 350°F, gas mark 4. Draw around the tin on some baking parchment with a pencil. Cut out the square.

2. Oil the insides of the tin. Put the square of paper inside the tin. Pour about 5cm (2in) of water into a pan and heat it.

3. When the water bubbles, take the pan off the heat. Put a heatproof bowl inside the pan and add the chocolate drops.

4. Stir the chocolate until it melts. Wearing oven gloves, lift the bowl from the pan. Break the eggs into a bowl and beat them.

5. Put the vanilla essence, butter and sugar into a bowl and beat them. Add the eggs, a little at a time, beating each time.

6. Sift both types of flour and the cocoa powder into the bowl. Add the melted chocolate and stir all the ingredients well.

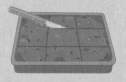

7. Chop the nuts then stir them into the mixture. Spoon the mixture into the tin. Smooth the top with the back of a spoon.

8. Bake the brownies for 35 minutes. They are ready when a crust has formed on top, but they are still soft in the middle.

9. Leave the brownies for 20 minutes, then cut them into squares. You could use a stencil to make icing sugar designs on top.

Bread rolls

To make 12 rolls, you will need:
450g (1lb) strong white bread flour
1 teaspoon of salt
2 teaspoons of dried easy-blend yeast
300ml (½ pint) warm water, which has been boiled
2 tablespoons of olive or vegetable oil
milk, for glazing
a greased baking tray

For the topping:
poppy, sesame or sunflower seeds, or rolled oats

Heat your oven to 220°C, 425°F, gas mark 7 in step 8.

❋ Eat on the day you make them, or store in an airtight
container and eat them within a day.

Use a wooden spoon.

1. Using a sieve, sift the flour and salt into a large bowl. Add the yeast and stir it in. Then, make a hollow in the middle.

2. Pour the warm water and oil into a jug. Pour them into the hollow, then stir everything well, to make a soft dough.

3. Put the dough onto a floury surface. Knead it by pressing your knuckles into the dough, then firmly pushing it away.

The warmth makes the dough rise to twice its original size.

4. Fold the dough, turn it around, then push it away again. Knead the dough for 10 minutes, until it is smooth and springy.

5. Put the dough into a clean bowl and cover it with plastic foodwrap. Put the bowl in a warm place for 1½ hours.

6. Sprinkle more flour on the work surface. Knead the dough for a minute to squeeze out any bubbles that have formed.

Grease the baking tray with oil.

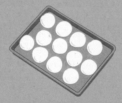

7. Break the dough into 12 pieces, then roll them into balls. Put the balls onto a baking tray, with spaces between them.

8. Put the rolls in a warm place and leave them for about 40 minutes to rise. After about 25 minutes, turn on your oven.

9. Brush the rolls with a little milk. Sprinkle them with a topping, then bake them for 12-15 minutes. Cool them on a wire rack.

Orange shortbread stars

Makes 14 biscuits

150g (5oz) plain flour
25g (1oz) semolina or ground rice
100g (4oz) chilled butter
1 small orange
50g (2oz) caster sugar

a 7½cm (3in) star-shaped cutter

✿ These will keep in an airtight
container for up to 4 days.

1. Heat the oven to 170°C, 325°F, gas mark 3. Wipe a little oil over two baking trays. Sift the flour into a large bowl.

2. Sift the semolina or ground rice into the bowl. Cut the butter into chunks. Put it in the bowl and coat it with flour.

3. Rub the butter between your fingertips. Lift it and let it fall back into the bowl as you rub, until it looks like fine breadcrumbs.

4. Use the medium holes of a grater to grate the rind of an orange onto a plate. Add the rind and the sugar to the mixture.

5. Cut the orange in half and squeeze one half. Sprinkle two teaspoons of juice over the mixture. Stir everything together.

6. Hold the bowl in one hand. Use your other hand to squeeze the dough into a ball. The heat from your hand makes it stick together.

7. Sprinkle flour onto a rolling pin and a clean surface. Put the dough on the surface and roll it out until it is 5mm (¼in) thick.

8. Use the cutter to cut out lots of stars from the dough. Use a spatula to lift them onto a tray. Squeeze the scraps together.

9. Roll out the dough and cut out more stars. Use a toothpick to press dots around the edges. Bake them for 12-15 minutes.

Jam-filled cookies

To make about 20 cookies, you will need:
100g (4oz) butter, softened
1 teaspoon of vanilla essence
50g (2oz) icing sugar
100g (4oz) plain flour
25g (1oz) cornflour
25g (1oz) desiccated coconut
seedless raspberry jam
two baking trays, wiped with cooking oil

Heat your oven to 180°C, 350°F,
gas mark 4, before you start.

🌸 Store in an airtight
container and eat
within 5 days.

Use a wooden spoon.

1. Put the butter into a large bowl and stir it until it is creamy. Then, add the vanilla essence and stir it in.

2. Sift the icing sugar through a sieve into the bowl. Then, stir the mixture well, until it is smooth and creamy.

3. Sift the flour and the cornflour into the bowl, then add the coconut. Stir everything well, to make a soft dough.

The balls of dough spread as they cook.

4. Sprinkle flour on your hands. Then, scoop up a little of the dough with a teaspoon and roll it into a smooth ball.

5. Make the rest of the mixture into balls, too. Then, put them all onto the baking trays, leaving spaces between them.

6. Push your little finger into the middle of each ball, to make a hollow. Push it up to the first knuckle, like this.

Wear oven gloves.

7. Bake the cookies for 12-14 minutes. Carefully lift them out of the oven, then leave them to cool on the baking trays.

8. When the cookies have cooled, sift a little icing sugar over them. Then, use a teaspoon to fill the holes with jam.

Pasta salad

To make a salad for 4 people, you will need:
300g (10oz) dried or 375g (12oz) fresh farfalle
175g (6oz) thin green beans
400g (14oz) can of tuna
10 cherry tomatoes

For the dressing:
4 tablespoons of mayonnaise
4 tablespoons of milk
a pinch of salt and of ground
   black pepper
4 fresh chives

❀ Store in a fridge and eat on
the day you make it.

Use clean kitchen scissors.

1. Half-fill a large saucepan with water. Heat it until it boils, then add the pasta and stir it with a wooden spoon.

2. Cook the pasta for as long as it says on the packet. Drain it through a colander, then tip it back into the pan to cool.

3. Mix a little butter into the pasta. Snip the ends off the beans and cut them in half. Then, half-fill a pan with water.

4. Boil the water, then add the beans. Cook the beans for 5 minutes, then drain them. Rinse them with cold water.

5. Open the can of tuna and drain it through a sieve. Put the tuna on a saucer and use a fork to break it up a little.

6. Cut the tomatoes in half. Then, put them into a large bowl with the pasta, beans and tuna. Mix everything well.

Use kitchen scissors.

7. For the dressing, put the mayonnaise, milk, salt and pepper into a bowl. Mix everything together with a fork.

8. Pour the dressing over the pasta mixture. Use a fork to toss the mixture in the dressing so all of the pieces are covered.

9. Cut the chives into tiny pieces, then scatter them over the salad. Serve the salad straight away or put it into a fridge.

Raspberry pastry swirls

To make about 40 swirls, you will need:
225g (8oz) ready-made puff pastry,
   cut from a block and taken out of the
   fridge 20 minutes before you start
icing sugar, for dusting
3 tablespoons of raspberry jam
1 tablespoon of caster sugar

Heat your oven to 200°C, 400°F,
gas mark 6 in step 6.

✿ Store in an airtight container
and eat within 5 days.

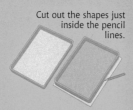

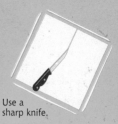

Use a sharp knife.

1. Lay two baking trays on baking parchment and draw around them. Cut out the shapes, then lay them in the trays.

2. Dust icing sugar onto a clean surface and a rolling pin. Then, roll out the pastry to a square as wide as the rolling pin.

3. Trim the edges of the pastry, so that they are straight. Then, cut the pastry down the middle to make two rectangles.

Roll the pastry tightly.

4. Spread half of the jam over each piece of pastry with a blunt knife. Leave a thin border around the edges of each piece.

5. Brush water along one edge of one piece, then roll the pastry from the opposite edge. Repeat this with the other piece.

6. Wrap the pastry rolls in plastic foodwrap, then chill them in a fridge for 30 minutes. While they chill, turn on your oven.

Use a sharp knife.

Wear oven gloves.

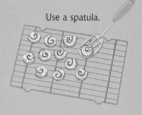

Use a spatula.

7. Unwrap the rolls, then cut them into slices about 1cm (½in) thick. Put the slices onto the baking trays and space them out.

8. Sprinkle half of the sugar on the swirls. Bake them for 10-12 minutes, until they are golden. Lift them out of the oven.

9. Sprinkle the rest of the sugar over the hot swirls. After 5 minutes, move them onto a wire rack and leave them to cool.

Tropical fruit loaf

To make about 10 slices, you will need:

1 large orange
175g (6oz) butter, softened
175g (6oz) caster sugar
3 medium eggs
100g (4oz) self-raising wholemeal flour
100g (4oz) plain flour
1 teaspoon of baking powder
250g (9oz) packet of chopped dried tropical fruit
a 900g (2lb) loaf tin, measuring about
   20.5 x 12.5 x 8cm (8 x 5 x 3½in)

For the icing:
75g (3oz) icing sugar

Heat your oven to 180°C, 350°F,
gas mark 4, before you start.

❀ Store in an airtight
container and eat
within 3 days.

Use the medium holes.

Pour the juice into a jug.

1. Grease the inside of the tin. Line the bottom with baking parchment. Then, grate the rind off the orange.

2. Squeeze the juice from the orange using a lemon squeezer. Put the rind, butter and sugar into a large bowl. Stir them well.

3. Break the eggs into a small bowl and mix them with a fork. Then, mix them into the creamy mixture, a little at a time.

Smooth the top with the back of the spoon.

4. Put both kinds of flour and the baking powder into a sieve. Then, gently shake the sieve, to sift them into the bowl.

5. Chop the fruit into small pieces. Put 25g (1oz) to one side. Add the rest to the bowl, with a tablespoon of the juice.

6. Gently turn the mixture over with a spoon, to mix everything well. Spoon it into the tin, then bake the loaf for 20 minutes.

Peel off the baking parchment.

Scatter the rest of the fruit over the top of the loaf.

7. Carefully lift the loaf out of the oven. Cover the top with foil and bake it for another 50 minutes. Then, lift it out.

8. Press the loaf with a finger. If it is firm, leave it in the tin for 15 minutes, then cool it on a wire rack. If not, cook it a little more.

9. Sift the icing sugar into a bowl and mix in a tablespoon of orange juice. Then, spread the icing over the loaf.

Tagliatelle carbonara

To make 4 servings, you will need:
150g (5oz) streaky bacon
2 whole cloves of garlic, peeled
1½ tablespoons of olive oil
50g (2oz) Parmesan cheese
3 medium eggs
2 tablespoons of fresh
parsley, chopped
3 tablespoons of single cream
a pinch of ground black pepper
350g (12oz) dried tagliatelle

✿ Eat the tagliatelle
straight away.

Add a teaspoon of olive oil, too.

Don't crush the garlic.

1. Half-fill a saucepan with water, then boil the water. Turn off the heat, then put the pan to one side until step 6.

2. Cut any rind off the bacon with clean kitchen scissors. Then, cut the bacon into strips and put them into a saucepan.

3. Add the garlic and 1½ tablespoons of oil. Heat the pan on a medium heat for 3-4 minutes, until the bacon is crispy.

4. Turn off the heat. Lift out the bacon with a spoon and put it onto some paper towels. Then, throw away the garlic.

5. Grate the cheese finely. Break the eggs into a bowl, then add half of the cheese, the parsley, cream and black pepper.

6. Mix everything with a fork. Boil the water in the pan again, then cook the tagliatelle for as long as it says on the packet.

The hot pasta cooks the egg.

7. Watch the pasta as it cooks. If it starts to boil too strongly, turn down the heat a little, but keep the water bubbling.

8. When it is cooked, turn off the heat. Drain the pasta through a colander, then tip it back into the pan and add the bacon.

9. Stir in the egg mixture really well, until there is no liquid egg left. Serve the pasta and sprinkle the rest of the cheese over it.

Iced raspberry mousse

To make 4 mousses, you will need:
150g (5oz) raspberries
4 tablespoons of icing sugar, sifted
4 tablespoons of Greek-style yogurt
150ml (¼ pint) double cream
25g (1oz) meringues (bought
  or home-made)
fresh raspberries and small mint
  leaves, to decorate
four 150ml (¼ pint) ramekin dishes

✿ You can store the mousses
in a freezer for up to a week.

1. Put the raspberries into a bowl. Mash them with a fork until they are squashed. Then, add the icing sugar to the bowl.

2. Mix the raspberries and icing sugar with a spoon. Then, add the yogurt and stir until everything is mixed well.

3. Pour the cream into a bowl. Then, whisk the cream, until it is thick and there are points when you lift the whisk.

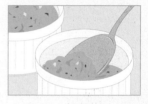

4. Add the yogurt mixture to the cream. Then, gently turn the mixture over and over with a spoon, to mix it.

5. Carry on until the mixture is pink. Break the meringues into small pieces, then add them and stir them in.

6. Spoon the mixture into the dishes. Put them into a freezer for 2 hours, or until the mousses are frozen solid.

7. Take the frozen mousses out of the freezer. Decorate each one with a raspberry and two mint leaves.

Fudgy banana muffins

Makes 12 muffins

250g (9oz) self-raising flour
1 teaspoon baking powder
100g (4oz) fudge
100g (4oz) soft light brown sugar
75g (3oz) butter
125ml (4½fl oz) milk
1 teaspoon vanilla essence
2 medium ripe bananas
2 medium eggs

2 tablespoons clear honey

a 12-hole muffin or deep bun tray
paper muffin cases

✿ These are best eaten on the day
you make them, but can be stored
in an airtight container in the fridge
for up to 3 days.

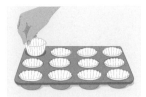

1. Heat the oven to 190ºC, 375ºF, gas mark 5. Line the tray with paper cases. Sift the flour and baking powder into a bowl.

2. Cut the fudge into chunks. Add the sugar and fudge to the bowl and stir. Make a hollow in the middle of the mixture.

3. Put the butter in a pan. Heat it gently until the butter melts. Take the pan off the heat. Add the milk and vanilla essence.

4. Peel the bananas and put them in a bowl. Mash them with a fork. Break the eggs into another bowl and beat them.

5. Add the bananas and the beaten eggs to the pan, then stir. Pour the mixture into the hollow in the dry ingredients.

6. Stir everything until it is just mixed together. The mixture should still look quite lumpy. Then, spoon it into the paper cases.

7. Bake the muffins for 20 minutes. Leave them for five minutes. Brush the tops with honey, then place them on a wire rack.

Spicy bean soup

To make soup for 4 people, you will need:
1 red onion
1 tablespoon of olive oil
1 clove of garlic, crushed
half a teaspoon of mild chilli powder
half a teaspoon of ground coriander
half a teaspoon of ground cumin
450ml (¾ pint) tomato juice
1 vegetable stock cube, mixed with
   450ml (¾ pint) of boiling water
a pinch of salt and of ground
   black pepper
400g (14oz) can of red kidney
   beans or mixed beans
1 tablespoon of chopped fresh
   coriander or parsley

❀ Eat straight away.

1. Peel the onion and cut it in half. Slice it finely, then chop it. Put the chopped onion and oil into a large saucepan.

2. Gently cook the onion on a low heat for 6-10 minutes, until it is soft. Stir it often, to stop it sticking to the pan.

3. Take the pan off the heat. Then, add the garlic, chilli powder, ground coriander and ground cumin.

4. Stir everything well, then heat the mixture gently for 1 minute. Stir it all the time, to stop the spices sticking.

5. Add the tomato juice, stock, salt and pepper. Drain the beans through a colander in the sink, then rinse them well.

6. Add the beans to the pan, then stir the soup and heat it until it boils. Then, reduce the heat so that it is bubbling gently.

Leave a small gap, to let out the steam.

Scoop up lots of beans with the ladle.

7. Put a lid onto the pan, then cook the soup for 15 minutes, stirring it often. Turn off the heat, then let it cool for 15 minutes.

8. Using a ladle, put half of the soup into a food processor. Blend it until it is smooth. Then, ladle the soup back into the pan.

9. Mix the soup in the pan, then heat it until it is bubbling gently. Stir in the chopped coriander or parsley, then serve it.

Chocolate log

Makes about 10 slices

For the cake:
4 large eggs
125g (5oz) caster sugar
60g (2½oz) ground almonds
1½ tablespoons cocoa powder
1¼ teaspoons baking powder

For the filling:
300ml (½ pint) double cream
1 tin of cherries

a 35 x 25cm (14 x 10in)
Swiss roll tin

❀ This will keep stored in
an airtight container in the
fridge for 2 days.

Sift more icing sugar over the
log before you serve it.

1. Heat the oven to 180ºC, 350ºF, gas mark 4. Grease and line the tin. Separate all the egg whites from the egg yolks.

2. Add the sugar to the bowl containing the yolks. Whisk them together. Stir in the ground almonds, cocoa and baking powder.

3. Whisk the egg whites with a whisk, until they are really thick. The egg whites should make stiff peaks, like this.

4. Spoon the egg whites into the yolk mixture. Fold them in until everything is mixed well. Pour the mixture into the tin.

5. Bake the cake for 20-25 minutes. Leave it to cool for ten minutes, then cover it with baking parchment and a cloth.

6. Put the tin in the fridge for two hours to chill. Meanwhile, pour the cream into a bowl and whisk it until it is just thick.

Use the parchment to help you roll up the cake.

7. Take the cake out of the fridge. Run a knife around the sides. Lay some baking parchment down and sift icing sugar onto it.

8. Turn the cake onto the parchment. Peel off the oily parchment. Spread the cream over the cake. Drain the cherry syrup.

9. Remove the cherry stones and scatter the cherries onto the cream. Roll up the cake from one of the short ends.

Jammy cut-out biscuits

Makes 10 biscuits

100g (4oz) butter, softened
50g (2oz) caster sugar
1 orange
1 medium egg
2 tablespoons ground almonds
   (optional)
200g (7oz) plain flour
1 tablespoon cornflour
8 tablespoons seedless
   raspberry jam

a 5cm (2in) round cutter
small shaped cutters

✿ Store in an airtight container
and eat within 2 days.

1. Heat the oven to 180°C, 350°F, gas mark 4. Grease two baking trays. Beat the butter and sugar in a large bowl, until they are creamy.

2. Grate the orange rind on the medium holes of a grater. Try not to grate the white part. Add the rind to the bowl and stir it in.

3. Break the egg into a cup and beat it with a fork, then add a little to the bowl. Mix it in. Add some more and mix that in.

4. Carry on until you have added all the egg. Add the ground almonds too, if you are using them. Sift in the flour and cornflour.

5. Use your hands to mix everything into a dough. Wrap it in plastic foodwrap. Put it in the fridge for 30 minutes to chill.

6. Sprinkle some flour onto a clean surface and a rolling pin. Roll out the dough until it is about 3mm (⅛ in) thick.

7. Using the round cutter, cut out lots of circles. Use the shaped cutters to cut holes in the middle of half the circles.

8. Squeeze the scraps into a ball, roll it out and cut more circles. Put all the circles on the trays. Bake the biscuits for 15 minutes.

9. Leave the biscuits for two minutes, then lift them onto a wire rack. Spread jam on the whole biscuits, then put a cut-out biscuit on top.

Potato and apple salad

To make a salad for 4 people, you will need:

For the lemon and honey dressing:
5 tablespoons of sunflower oil
1½ tablespoons of lemon juice
1 teaspoon of clear honey
a pinch of salt and of ground black pepper

For the salad:
750g (1lb 10oz) small new potatoes
2 sticks of celery
2 small dessert apples
6 fresh chives

❁ Eat straight away.

Screw on the lid before you shake the jar.

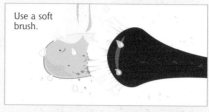
Use a soft brush.

1. For the dressing, put the oil, lemon juice, honey, salt and pepper into a jar with a screw top. Shake the jar well, to mix the dressing.

2. Scrub the potatoes clean. Half-fill a pan with water and heat it until the water boils. Add the potatoes and boil them for 15-20 minutes.

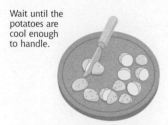
Wait until the potatoes are cool enough to handle.

3. Carefully pour the potatoes into a colander to drain them. Leave them to cool a little, then cut the potatoes in half.

4. Put the potatoes into a large bowl. Pour the dressing over them while they are still warm, then leave them to cool completely.

Use a sharp knife.

5. Wash the celery and cut it into thin slices. Then, cut the apples into quarters and cut out the cores. Cut the apples into small chunks.

6. Using kitchen scissors, snip the chives into small pieces. Add the celery, apples and chives to the bowl, then mix everything well.

Flower sweets

To make about 40 flower sweets, you will need:
225g (8oz) icing sugar
1 tablespoon of lemon juice
(from a bottle or squeezed from a lemon)
2 teaspoons of egg white, mixed from dried
egg white (mix as directed on the packet)
2-3 drops of lemon essence
small jelly sweets
a small flower-shaped cutter

❀ Store the flower sweets in an airtight
  container, on layers of greaseproof
  paper. Eat them within a week.

1. Lay a baking tray on a piece of greaseproof paper and draw around it. Cut out the shape and put it into the tin.

2. Sift the icing sugar through a sieve into a large bowl. Make a hollow in the middle of the icing sugar with a spoon.

3. Mix the lemon juice, egg white and lemon essence in a small bowl. Pour the mixture into the hollow in the sugar.

If the mixture is a little dry, add a drop of water.

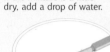

4. Stir everything with a blunt knife until a ball starts to form. Squeeze the mixture with your fingers until it is smooth.

5. Sprinkle a little icing sugar onto a clean work surface. Sprinkle some onto a rolling pin too, to stop the mixture sticking.

6. Roll out the mixture on the work surface until it is about 5mm (¼in) thick. Then, use the cutter to cut out a flower shape.

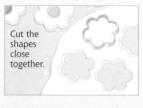

Cut the shapes close together.

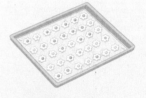

7. Put a sweet onto the middle of the flower, and press it. Then, lift the flower onto the baking tray with a blunt knife.

8. Cut out more flowers and press sweets onto them. If a sweet won't stick, dab water on the flower, then press it on.

9. Press the scraps into a ball. Roll it out and make more flowers, then leave them on the baking tray for 2 hours to harden.

Stripy marzipan canes

To make 4 canes, you will need:
90g (3½oz) 'white' marzipan*,
  cut from a block
red food colouring

✿ Store the canes in an
airtight container and eat
them within 3 weeks.

*Marzipan
contains ground
nuts, so don't give the
canes to anyone who
is allergic to nuts.

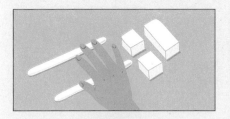

1. Cut the piece of marzipan into three pieces the same size. Then, cut two of the pieces in half and roll them to make sticks.

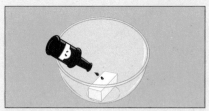

2. Put the remaining piece of marzipan into a small bowl. Add 3 drops of red food colouring and mix it in with your fingers.

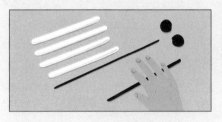

3. Break the red marzipan into four pieces. Then, roll each piece into a thin stick, about three times as long as your middle finger.

Hold this end as you wind.

4. Starting at one end, wind a red stick around a white one, like this. Do this with all the sticks, to make three more stripy sticks.

5. Roll the sticks on a clean work surface, to make them smooth. Then, bend the end of each one into a curve, to make a cane.

To make pink stripy canes, use pink colouring instead of red.

Spaghetti bolognese

To make spaghetti bolognese for 4 people,
you will need:

1 onion
1 carrot
1 stick of celery
2 tablespoons of olive oil
1 clove of garlic, crushed
450g (1lb) minced beef
1 beef or vegetable stock cube
300ml (½ pint) boiling water
400g (14oz) can of chopped tomatoes
1 teaspoon of dried mixed herbs
1 tablespoon of tomato purée
2 pinches of salt and of ground
  black pepper
400g (14oz) dried spaghetti

Serve with grated Parmesan
cheese sprinkled over the top.

✿ Eat straight away.

182

Cut the ends off the carrot.

Throw away the ends of the celery.

Use a wooden spoon.

1. Peel the onion, cut it in half and chop it finely. Peel the carrot with a potato peeler. Cut it in half, then chop it finely.

2. Slice and chop the celery. Put the onion and oil into a large saucepan. Cook them on a medium heat for 5 minutes.

3. Add the garlic, carrot and celery. Cook all the vegetables for 2 minutes, stirring them all the time. Then, add the beef.

Stir the beef all the time.

4. Cook the beef for about 10 minutes, or until it is brown all over. Break up any lumps with the wooden spoon.

5. Put the stock cube into a heatproof jug. Add the boiling water and stir it until the cube dissolves. Add the stock to the pan.

6. Add the tomatoes, herbs, tomato purée, salt and pepper. Boil the sauce, then reduce the heat, so that it is bubbling gently.

Leave a small gap, to let out the steam.

Carefully push the spaghetti into the water.

7. Put a lid onto the pan. Cook the sauce for 40 minutes, stirring it often. Remove the lid and cook it for 10 more minutes.

8. While the sauce is cooking, boil a saucepan of water. Then, cook the spaghetti according to the instructions on the packet.

9. Drain the spaghetti through a colander. Spoon it into bowls, then spoon the bolognese sauce over the top.

Lemon layer cake

❀ This will keep for 2-3 days in an airtight container in the fridge.

Makes 10 slices

1 lemon
225g (8oz) self-raising flour
1 teaspoon baking powder
4 medium eggs
225g (8oz) soft margarine
225g (8oz) caster sugar

For the lemon curd filling:
2 medium eggs
75g (3oz) caster sugar
1 lemon
50g (2oz) unsalted butter

For the lemon icing:
1 lemon
125g (5oz) icing sugar

three 20cm (8in) round,
shallow cake tins

1. Heat the oven to 180°C, 350°F, gas mark 4. Grease and line three tins. Grate the rind of a lemon. Then, juice the lemon.

2. Sift the flour and baking powder into a bowl. Stir in the margarine and sugar. Break the eggs into a cup, then beat them in too.

3. Stir in the lemon juice and rind. Split the mixture between the tins and bake for 20 minutes. Turn the cakes out onto a wire rack.

4. For the filling, break the eggs into a heatproof bowl and beat them. Add the sugar, lemon rind and the juice of a lemon.

5. Cut the butter into chunks and add them. Put 5cm (2in) water into a pan. Heat it until it bubbles. Put the bowl into the pan.

6. Stir the mixture as it thickens. After 20 minutes, the mixture should coat the back of a spoon. Take the pan off the heat.

Don't worry if some filling oozes out.

Use a zester if you have one.

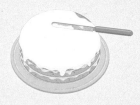

7. Spread a cake with half the filling. Put another cake on top. Spread the rest of the filling over that cake. Put the final cake on top.

8. Grate the rind of a lemon. For the icing, squeeze the juice from half of the lemon. Sift the icing sugar into a bowl.

9. Stir the lemon juice into the icing until it is smooth. Spread the icing over the cake. Sprinkle the rind on top of the cake.

Peppermint creams

To make about 40 peppermint creams, you will need:
250g (9oz) icing sugar
2½ teaspoons of egg white, mixed from dried
  egg white (mix as directed on the packet)
1 teaspoon of peppermint flavouring
2 teaspoons of lemon juice
red and green food colouring
small cutters
a baking tray

✿ Store in an airtight container
and eat within a week.

1. Sift the icing sugar through a sieve into a large bowl. Then, make a hollow in the middle of the sugar with a spoon.

2. Mix the egg white, peppermint and lemon juice in a small bowl. Pour the mixture into the hollow in the icing sugar.

3. Stir the mixture with a blunt knife, then squeeze it with your fingers until it is smooth. Cut it into two equal halves.

Add a little icing sugar if the mixture is sticky.

4. Put each half into a bowl. Add a few drops of red food colouring to one, then add green colouring to the other.

5. Using your fingers, mix the red colouring into the icing sugar. Wash your hands, then mix in the green colouring.

6. Sprinkle a little icing sugar over a clean surface and a rolling pin. This will help to stop the mixture sticking to them.

Cut the shapes close together.

Use a blunt knife.

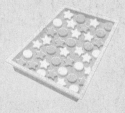

7. Roll out the pink mixture, until it is about 5mm (¼in) thick. Then, use the cutters to cut out lots of little shapes.

8. Lift the shapes onto the baking tray. Squash the scraps into a ball and roll them out again. Cut out more shapes.

9. Cut out green shapes and put them onto the baking tray, too. Leave the peppermint creams for an hour to harden.

Italian tomato salad

To make salads for 4 people,
you will need:
4 large ripe tomatoes
4 tablespoons of olive oil
salt and ground black pepper
300g (10oz) mozzarella cheese
8 large fresh basil leaves

❀ Chill in the refrigerator for 30
minutes, then eat straight away.

1. Using a serrated knife, cut the tomatoes in half and cut out their cores. Lay each half on its flat side, then slice them as finely as you can.

2. Arrange the tomatoes on four plates. Drizzle a tablespoon of oil over each serving, then sprinkle with a pinch of salt and of pepper, too.

3. If the mozzarella cheese is in a bag full of liquid, cut it open and pour away the liquid. Then, cut the mozzarella into thin slices.

4. Lay the slices of mozzarella amongst the sliced tomatoes. Then, tear the basil leaves into thin strips and sprinkle them over the top.

5. Cover the plates with plastic foodwrap and put them into a fridge for about 30 minutes. Then, unwrap them and serve.

Plum tarts

Makes 14 tarts

375g (13oz) packet of
   ready-rolled puff pastry
300g (12oz) red plums
1 thick slice white bread
50g (2oz) butter
50g (2oz) soft light brown sugar
½ teaspoon ground mixed spice
4 tablespoons apricot jam

6½cm (2½in) round cutter

You could sieve some icing
sugar over the tarts.

✿ Store in a single layer in an
airtight container in the fridge.
Eat within a day or two.

1. Heat the oven to 220ºC, 425ºF, gas mark 7. Take the pastry from the fridge and leave it for 15-20 minutes. Cut the plums in half.

2. Remove the stones, then cut the plums into chunks. Put the chunks into a bowl. Grate the bread into breadcrumbs.

3. Gently heat the butter in a small frying pan until it has just melted. Pour half of the melted butter into a small bowl.

4. Turn up the heat a little. Add the breadcrumbs to the frying pan. Fry them for about five minutes, stirring them often.

5. Remove the pan from the heat. When the breadcrumbs are cool, use your hands to mix in the plums, sugar and spice.

6. Unroll the pastry. Use the cutter to cut out 14 circles. Put the circles on the baking trays, then prick each circle with a fork.

7. Brush some butter from the bowl around the edge of each circle. Spoon some jam into the middle of each one.

8. Spoon some plums onto the jam. Bake the tarts for 12-15 minutes. Remove them from the oven and put them on a wire rack.

Gingerbread flowers

Makes 25 biscuits

350g (12oz) plain flour
1 teaspoon bicarbonate of soda
½ teaspoon ground cinnamon
1½ teaspoons ground ginger
100g (4oz) chilled butter
175g (6oz) light muscovado sugar
1 medium egg
2 tablespoons golden syrup
writing icing

a flower-shaped cookie cutter

❀ Store in an airtight container, in a
single layer or with baking parchment
between the layers, and eat within 2 days.

1. Heat the oven to 180°C, 350°F, gas mark 4. Wipe a little oil over two baking trays. Use a sieve to sift the flour into a bowl.

2. Sift the bicarbonate of soda, cinnamon and ginger into the bowl. Cut the butter into chunks and stir it into the flour.

3. Use your fingertips to rub the butter into the flour, until the mixture looks like breadcrumbs. Stir in the sugar.

4. Break the egg into a bowl and beat it with a fork. Add the syrup and beat it. Add the mixture to the flour and mix it in.

5. Use your hands to squeeze the mixture, until it becomes a smooth dough. Cut the dough in half with a blunt knife.

6. Sprinkle flour on a clean work surface and put one piece of dough onto it. Roll it out until it is about 5mm (¼in) thick.

7. Use a cookie cutter to cut lots of shapes from the dough. Use a spatula to lift them onto the baking trays.

8. Roll out the rest of the dough. Cut out more shapes. Bake them in the oven for 12-15 minutes. Leave them for 5 minutes.

9. Use a spatula to lift the biscuits onto a wire rack. When they are cool, draw patterns on them with writing icing.

Little cheese scones

To make about 16 scones, you will need:
40g (1½oz) Cheddar cheese
175g (6oz) self-raising flour
half a level teaspoon of baking powder
a pinch of salt
25g (1oz) butter
100ml (4fl oz) milk
milk, for glazing
4cm (1½in) round and heart-shaped cutters
a greased baking tray

Heat your oven to 220°C, 425°F,
gas mark 7, before you start.

✿ Eat straight away or store in an airtight
container and eat within 3 days.

 Use the medium holes.

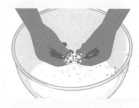

1. Grate the cheese using a grater. Then, sift the flour, baking powder and salt through a sieve into a large bowl.

2. Cut the butter into small pieces and add it to the bowl. Rub it in, until the mixture looks like fine breadcrumbs.

3. Mix in the grated cheese with your hands. Pour in the milk, then use a blunt knife to mix everything well.

4. Gently squeeze the mixture with your hands to make a soft dough. Then, sprinkle some flour onto a clean work surface.

5. Using a rolling pin, roll out the dough until it is about 1cm (½in) thick. Then, use the cutters to cut out circles and hearts.

6. Squeeze the scraps of dough into a ball and roll them out again. Then, cut out lots more circles and hearts.

The scones will rise and turn golden.

You could sprinkle some of the scones with a little plain flour or grated cheese before they are baked.

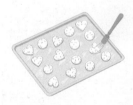

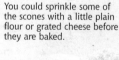

7. Put the shapes onto the baking tray, leaving spaces between them. Then, brush a little milk over the tops of them.

8. Bake the scones for 7-8 minutes. Wearing oven gloves, lift them out of the oven. Put them onto a wire rack to cool.

Sticky chocolate cake

To make about 8 slices of cake,
you will need:

200g (7oz) self-raising flour
half a teaspoon of baking powder
4 tablespoons of cocoa powder
4 medium eggs
225g (8oz) soft margarine
225g (8oz) light soft brown sugar
1 tablespoon of milk
two 20cm (8in) round cake tins

For the sticky chocolate icing:
150g (5oz) plain chocolate
150ml (¼ pint) double cream

Heat your oven to 180°C, 350°F,
gas mark 4 in step 4.

Take the eggs and margarine out
of the fridge half an hour before
you start.

✿ Store the cake in an
airtight container in a fridge
and eat it within 2 days.

Use a heatproof bowl.

Keep stirring until the chocolate has melted.

1. Break the chocolate into pieces and put them into a bowl with the cream. Fill a saucepan a quarter full of water.

2. Heat the water until it bubbles, then take the pan off the heat. Put the bowl into it, then stir the chocolate and cream.

3. Let the icing cool for a few minutes, then put it into a fridge for at least an hour. Stir it every now and then, as it thickens.

Use a paper towel.

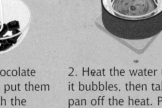

Cut out the circles just inside the pencil lines.

Stir the mixture until it is smooth.

4. While the icing thickens, turn on your oven. Wipe cooking oil over the inside of each tin, then lay the tins on greaseproof paper.

5. Draw around the tins, cut out the circles and lay them in the tins. Sift the flour, baking powder and cocoa into a large bowl.

6. Break the eggs into a mug. Add them to the large bowl, then add the margarine, sugar and milk. Stir everything well.

Press the middle – if it is springy, the cake is cooked.

Loosen the edges of the cakes with a blunt knife.

7. Spoon the mixture into the tins and smooth the tops. Bake the cakes for about 25 minutes, then carefully lift them out.

8. Leave the cakes in the tins for 5 minutes. Turn them out onto a wire rack. Peel off the paper and leave them to cool.

9. Spread some icing on the top of one cake, then lay the other cake on top. Spread the rest of the icing all over the outside.

Raspberry and almond cake

Makes 10 slices

For the cake:
4 medium eggs
165g (5½oz) caster sugar
225g (8oz) ground almonds
1 teaspoon baking powder

For the filling:
150g (5oz) seedless raspberry jam
150g (5oz) fresh raspberries

For the icing:
200g (7oz) icing sugar
2 tablespoons warm water
a handful of raspberries to
    decorate

a 20 cm (8in) round cake tin,
    about 7½cm (3in) deep

✿ This will keep stored in an airtight
container in the fridge for 2 days.

1. Heat the oven to 170ºC, 325ºF or gas mark 3. Grease and line the tin. Break one egg into a bowl. Pour it onto a small plate.

2. Hold an egg cup over the yolk. Tip the plate over a bowl, so the egg white slides into it. Separate the rest of the eggs.

3. Add the sugar to the yolks and beat them together until they are paler. Whisk the egg whites until they are stiff.

4. When the egg whites form stiff peaks, add them to the yolk mixture. Use a metal spoon to gently fold them into the mixture.

5. Mix in the almonds and baking powder. Pour the mixture into the tin and bake it in the oven for 35-40 minutes.

6. Leave the cake in the tin for 20 minutes. Then, run a knife around the sides. Turn the cake out onto a wire rack.

7. To cut the cake in half horizontally, steady the cake with your hand. Then, using a bread knife, carefully cut the cake.

8. Beat the jam in a bowl. Mix in the raspberries. Spread the filling over the bottom half of the cake, then replace the top half.

9. Sift the icing sugar into a bowl, then stir in the water. Spread the icing over the cake, then decorate with raspberries.

Dainty sandwiches

To make 2 sandwiches, you will need:
4 slices of bread
thin slices of ham
butter or margarine
strawberry, raspberry or apricot jam
a large round cutter and a small cutter

✿ Eat the sandwiches straight away, or wrap them in plastic foodwrap and store them in a fridge for up to 6 hours.

1. Lay a slice of bread on a chopping board. Lay the round cutter on top of it and press hard. Then, remove the cut-out circle.

2. Cut another circle from a second slice of bread in the same way. Then, use the small cutter to cut a shape in one of the circles.

3. For the sandwich filling, lay the round cutter on a slice of ham. Then, very carefully cut around the cutter with a sharp knife.

4. Spread butter on one side of each bread circle. Lay the ham on the whole circle, then lay the circle with the hole on top of the ham.

You could also make cheese or cucumber sandwiches.

5. Cut two bread circles and cut a hole in one of them. Spread butter and jam on the whole circle, then press the circle with the hole on top.

Sweet pastry

Makes enough pastry to line a
   20cm (8in) flan tin

175g (6oz) plain flour
25g (1oz) icing sugar
100g (4oz) chilled butter
1 medium egg
2 teaspoons cold water

Baking beans, or a packet of dried
   beans or peas

1. Sift the flour and icing sugar through a sieve into a large bowl. Then, cut the butter into cubes and stir them in.

2. Rub the butter into the flour with the tips of your fingers. Carry on rubbing until the mixture looks like fine breadcrumbs.

You will not need the egg white in this recipe.

3. Break the egg onto a saucer. Hold an egg cup over the yolk and tip the saucer over a bowl, so the white slides into it.

4. Put the yolk in a small bowl with the water. Mix them with a fork. Then, sprinkle them over the mixture in the large bowl.

5. Stir the mixture until everything starts to stick together. Squeeze the pastry together to make a firm dough.

6. Sprinkle a little flour over a clean work surface. Lift the pastry onto the surface and pat it into a smooth ball.

7. Wrap the pastry in plastic foodwrap. Then, put it in the fridge for 30 minutes. This makes it easier to roll out flat.

Lining a pastry case

Turn the pastry a quarter of
the way around.

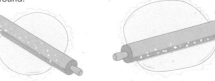

1. Put the pastry onto a
floury surface. Sprinkle
flour onto a rolling pin.
Roll over the pastry
once, then turn it.

2. Roll over and turn the
pastry again and again.
Carry on until the pastry
is slightly bigger than the
flan tin.

Be careful not to make
any holes in the pastry.

The rolling pin cuts off
any extra pastry.

'Blind' baking

The holes stop the
pastry rising up.

3. Roll the pastry around
the rolling pin. Lift it up
and unroll it over the tin.
Gently push the pastry
into the edges of the tin.

4. Roll the rolling pin over
the tin. Then, cover the
pastry case with plastic
foodwrap and put it in the
fridge for 20 minutes.

1. Put a baking tray into
the oven. Heat the oven
to 200°C, 400°F, gas
mark 6. Then, prick the
pastry base with a fork.

Try not to squash the pastry.

2. Cut a large square of
kitchen foil and gently
press it into the pastry
case. Then, fill the foil
with baking beans.

3. Lift out the hot baking
tray and put the flan tin
on it. Put it back into the
oven and bake the pastry
case for 8 minutes.

4. Carefully remove the
hot foil and beans. Then,
bake the empty case for
another 5 minutes, or
until it is pale golden.

Index

Written by Fiona Watt, Rebecca Gilpin,
Fiona Patchett, Leonie Pratt and Catherine Atkinson.

Designed & illustrated by Antonia Miller,
Non Figg, Nancy Leschnikoff, Nicola Butler,
Josephine Thompson, Helen Wood and Molly Sage.

This edition published in 2012 by Usborne Publishing Ltd,
83-85 Saffron Hill, London, EC1N 8RT, England. www.usborne.com